Sweet Love Stories

Norma Iris Pagan Morales

ISBN 978-1-959895-88-6 (paperback)
ISBN 978-1-959895-87-9 (ebook)

Printed in the United States of America

Dedication

This book is dedicated to my dear sister, Adelin M. Pagan Morales. She was not just my sister; she was also my best friend. She is gone now; however, she lives very deep in my heart.

My mini biography

The slogan of my life is too many stories and too little time to write. You are going to see that as an educator, I love giving explanations and definitions on every piece I write. Why do I do this? Well, when I was in grammar school and then college, I noticed that there was a lack of explanation on anything I read. Half of the time I was lost.

I had problems with my professors because they informed me that if I wanted to be an English teacher, it would be my job to explain each poem or story to my students.

Seriously, just look at all the books that I have written, and you will understand me better.

I'm a fool for romance stories. You will see it make an appearance in some of my writings.

I want to tell all my readers that I love dogs. I have two, however, I want to talk about one. Its name is Titi. She is smarter than most people I know though she doesn't look it.

My dog, Titi, is a genius! When I write a new story, I would read it at loud. Titi would sit there and wag its tail. If the story is boring, I see no reaction whatsoever.

Another thing that I must tell you is that I have found true love. Its name is chocolate ice cream!

Like all true love, it's love and hate. My body loves it, and my self-esteem hates it. I am just joking. All this might trickle down into my stories.

Some people may say I kid a lot but believe me that this is the main reason I am so unique....

Overview

How many people can really bring back the romance of their teenage love? Can you ever forget your high school love? Can that spark come alive when you see each other after twenty or thirty years?

Teenage love is something that packs enough innocent charm to make even the coldest hearts go warm. It is love in its most pure, immaculate, and unspoiled form because it is the first time ever in life that the heart has blossomed to love.

As adults, we observe love as something more complex than it is, however, during the teenage years, it is just a simple sensation of caring for someone else.

Many may argue that teenage love is ignorant, but hey, ignorance is heaven. Am I right?

Foreword

Short stories are pieces of prose fiction that can be read in one sit.
Oral storytelling traditions have been in fashion since the 17th century. They have grown to cover a body of work so varied as to challenge easy characterization.

At its most ideal, the short story features a small cast of named characters. Its intention is to focus on a self-contained incident by suggesting a single effect to capture an audience.

By doing so, short stories make use of plot, quality, and other dynamic components to a far greater degree than is typical tale. I want to bring out that a short story is far lesser degree than a novel.

Although the short story is largely distinct from the novel, authors of both generally are lured from a common pool of literary techniques.

Short stories have no set length. In terms of word count, there is no official separation between an anecdote, a short story, and a novel.

The form parameters of a tale or short story are given by the rhetorical. Also, the length depends on its the context in which a given story is produced and considered. What constitutes a short story may differ between genres, countries, eras, and commentators.

Like the novel, the short story's predominant shape reflects the demands of the available markets for publication. The writer must keep in mind the evolution and the form. The demands and evolution of a short story seems closely tied to the evolution of the publishing industry. The submission guidelines of its constituent houses also would make a difference.

The short story has been considered both an apprenticeship form preceding more lengthy works, and a crafted form, collected in books of similar length, price, and distribution to novels.

Short story writers may define their works as part of the artistic and personal expression of the form. They may also attempt to resist categorization by genre and fixed formation.

SHORT STORIES VS. NOVELS

The Length

Determining what exactly separates a short story from longer fictional formats is very problematic…

A classic definition of a short story is that one should be able to read it in one sitting. This point most notably was made in Edgar Allan Poe's essay "The Philosophy of Composition" in 1846.

Interpreting this standard nowadays is problematic, because the expected length of "one sitting" may now be briefer than it was in Poe's era. Other definitions place the maximum word count of the short story at anywhere from 1,000 to 4,000.

In contemporary usage, the term short story most often refers to a work of fiction no shorter than 1,000 and no longer than 20,000 words. Stories of fewer than 1,000 words are sometimes referred to as "short stories", or "flash fiction".

As a point of reference for the genre writer, the Science Fiction and Fantasy Writers of America define short story length in the Nebula Awards for science fiction submission guidelines as having a word count of fewer than 7,500 words.

Longer stories that cannot be called novels are sometimes considered "novellas" or novelettes. Short stories may be collected into the more marketable form of "collections". They often contain previously unpublished stories. Sometimes, authors who do not have the time or money to write a novella or novel decide to write short stories instead'.

They work out a deal with some popular magazines to publish them for profit.

Characteristics of a Short Story

As a concentrated form of narrative prose fiction, the short story has been theorized through the traditional elements of dramatic structure:

1. The event that introduces the conflict
    Is the exposition, the introduction of setting, situation and main characters, complication.
2. The decisive moment for the protagonist and his commitment to a course of action
    The rising action and crisis of the story.
3. The point of highest interest in terms of the conflict and the point with the most action
    The climax
4. The point when the conflict is resolved
    The resolution

Because of their length, short stories may or may not follow this pattern. For example, modern short stories only occasionally have an exposition, more typically beginning in the middle of the action. As with longer stories, plots of short stories also have a climax, crisis, or turning point. However, the endings of many short stories are abrupt and open. It may or may not have a moral or practical lesson. As with any art form, the exact characteristics of a short story will vary by the author.

Short stories tend to be less complex than novels?

Usually, a short story focuses on one incident; has a single plot, a single setting, and a small number of characters. It may cover a short period of time. The modern short story form emerged from oral story-telling traditions, the brief moralistic narratives of parables and fables.

The prose anecdote and all of these being forms of a swiftly sketched situation come quickly to its point.

The History of Short Stories

With the rise of the realistic novel, the short story evolved in a parallel tradition. Its first distinctive examples may be seen in the tales of E. T. A. Hoffmann. The character of the form developed particularly with authors known for their short fiction, by choice.

They wrote nothing else or by critical regard. It acknowledged the focus and craft required in a short form.

An example is Jorge Luis Borges, who won American fame with "The Garden of Forking Paths". This was published in the August 1948 Ellery Queen's Mystery Magazine.

Facts about Jorge Luis Borges
Jorge Luis Borges died at 86 years old
Born: August 24, 1899
Died: June 14, 1986
Birthplace: Buenos Aires, Argentina
Best known as: Author of the short story collection "Ficciones"

Another example is O. Henry, author of "Gift of the Magi", for whom the O. Henry Award is named.

Facts about O. Henry
Born: September 11, 1862
Died: June 5, 1910 (cirrhosis of the liver)
Birthplace: Greensboro, North Carolina, United States
Best known as: American short story writer
Name at birth: William Sydney Porter

O. Henry was the fictitious name of William Sydney Porter, who wrote colorful short stories with surprising and ironic twists. His best-known titles included:

"The Last of the Troubadours,"
"The Gift of the Magi"
"The Ransom of Red Chief"

Porter grew up in North Carolina but moved to Texas in the 1880s. He worked as a draftsman, a bookkeeper, a bank teller, and a newspaper columnist until 1898.

In 1898, Porter was sent to prison for embezzlement from his days as a teller in Austin Texas.

After more than three years in jail, O. Henry moved to New York to work full-time as a writer. His short stories were masterworks of careful plotting and surprise endings.

In "The Ransom of Red Chief", for instance, a kidnapped child is a troublemaker that the kidnappers ended up paying the boy's father to take him back.

O. Henry's work appeared in magazines and journals across the country. They were collected in such books as:

Cabbages and Kings in 1904
Heart of the West in 1907
The Voice of the City 1908

Other of his most popular, inventive, and most often reprinted stories, among over six hundred include:

1. A Municipal Report.
2. An Unfinished Story,
3. A Blackjack Barginer
4. A Lick penny Lover,

5. Mammon and the Archer
6. Two Thanksgiving Day Gentlemen
7. The Last Leaf

O. Henry was no stranger to alcohol and plagued. He got very sick and died broke at the age of 47.

The following is a list of some American Writers

1. Jack London,
2. Ambrose Bierce,
3. F. Scott Fitzgerald,
4. Ernest Hemingway,
5. William Faulkner,
6. Flannery O'Connor,
7. John Cheever
8. Raymond Carver

Science fiction short story with a special poetic touch was a genre developed with great popular success by Ray Bradbury. The genre of the short story was often neglected until the second half of the 19th century.

The evolution of printing technologies and periodical editions were among the factors contributing to the increasing importance of short story publications.

The following listing is about the pioneers in finding the rules of the genre in the Western canon:

Rudyard Kipling of United Kingdom
Anton Chekhov of Russia
Guy de Maupassant of France
Manuel Gutiérrez Nájera of Mexico
Rubén Darío of Nicaragua

An important theoretical example for storytelling analysis was provided by Walter Benjamin in his illuminated essay "The Storyteller". In that essay, he argued about the decline of storytelling art and the incommunicability of experiences in the modern world.

Oscar Wilde's essay "The Decay of Lying" and Henry James's "The Art of Fiction" are also partly related with this subject.

The Pioneers in storytellers

Short stories are dated back to oral storytelling traditions. They originally produced epics such as "Homer's Iliad and Odyssey".

The stories, that were oral narratives, were often told in the form of rhyming or rhythmic verses. Very often, they included frequent sections. As in the case of Homer, Homeric shows you so that can see those verses. Such stylistic devices often acted as reminders for easier recall, version, and adaptation of the story.

The short sections of verse might focus on individual narratives that could be told in just one sitting. The overall arc of the tale would emerge only through the telling of multiple sections.

The other ancient form of short story or the anecdote, was popular under the Roman Empire. Anecdotes functioned as a sort of parable, which is a brief realistic narrative that embodies a point.

Many surviving Roman anecdotes were collected in the 13th or 14th century as the Gesta Romanorum. Anecdotes remained popular in Europe well into the 18th century. That was when the fictional anecdotal letters of Sir Roger de Coverley were published.

In Europe, the oral story-telling tradition began to develop into written stories in the early 14th century. It was most notably with Geoffrey Chaucer's Canterbury Tales and Giovanni Boccaccio's Decameron.

Let me remind you that both books are composed of individual short stories. It ranges from farce or humorous anecdotes to well-crafted literary fictions. They are set within a larger narrative story. The frame-tale device was not adopted by all writers.

At the end of the 16th century, some of the most popular short stories in Europe were the darkly tragic "novella" of Matteo Bandello. You can see this especially in their French translation.

By the mid-17th century, in France, the development of a refined short novel, the "nouvelle", was seen by some authors as Madame de Lafayette.

In the 1690s, traditional fairy tales began to be published. One of the most famous collections was by Charles Perrault. The appearance of Antoine Galland's first modern translation of the Thousand and One Nights or Arabian Nights in the year 1704.

Other translations appeared during 1710 thru 1712. It had an enormous influence on the 18th-century European short stories of Voltaire, Diderot, and others.

EARLY PUBLISHED SHORT STORIES 1790–1850

There are early examples of short stories published separately between 1790 and 1810. However, the first true collections of short stories appeared from 1810 thru 1830 in several countries around the same period.

The first short stories in the United Kingdom were gothic tales like Richard Cumberland's "remarkable narrative" "The Poisoner of Montremos" in 1791.

Great novelists like Sir Walter Scott and Charles Dickens also wrote some short stories.

In the United States

One of the earliest short stories in the United States was Charles Brockden Brown's "Somnambulism" in 1805.

Washington Irving wrote mysterious tales including "Rip van Winkle" in 1819 and "The Legend of Sleepy Hollow" in 1820.

Nathaniel Hawthorne published the first part of his Twice-Told Tales in 1837.

Edgar Allan Poe wrote his tales of mystery and imagination between 1832 and 1849.

His Classic stories are:

"The Fall of the House of Usher"
"The Tell-Tale Heart"
"The Cask of Amontillado"
"The Pit and the Pendulum"
His first detective story, "The Murders in the Rue Morgue".

In "The Philosophy of Composition" in 1846. Poe argued that a literary work should be short enough for a reader to finish in one sitting.

A brief history of Edgar Allan Poe

Occupation- an American writer, poet, critic, and editor best known for evocative short stories and poems
Birth Date- January 19, 1809
Death Date- October 7, 1849

Edgar Allan Poe's imaginative storytelling and tales of mystery and horror gave birth to the modern detective story. "POE THE FATHER OF DECTIVE STORIES"
Poe married his cousin Virginia when she was 13 and he was 24.
Despite his awards and recognition, Poe had financial problems
Poe died in a Baltimore hospital in 1849. His last words were "Lord, help my poor soul."
Education
U.S. Military Academy at West Point, University of Virginia
Place of Birth
Boston, Massachusetts

Place of Death
Baltimore, Maryland

GERMANY

In Germany, the first collection of short stories was by Heinrich von Kleist in 1810 and 1811. The Brothers Grimm published their first volume of collected fairy tales in 1812.

E. T. A. Hoffmann followed with his own original fantasy tales, in "The Nutcracker and The Mouse King" in 181 are the most famous.

FRANCE

In France, Prosper Mérimée wrote Mateo Falcone in 1829

THE GROWTH OF PRINT MAGAZINES AND JOURNAL

1850–1900

In the latter half of the 19th century, the growth of print magazines and journals created a strong demand for short fiction of between 3,000 and 15,000 words.

In the United Kingdom, Thomas Hardy wrote dozens of short stories, included:

"The Three Strangers" in 1883

"A Mere Interlude" in 1885

"Barbara of the House of Grebe" in 1890

Rudyard Kipling published short story collections for grown-ups, e.g. Plain Tales from the Hills in 1888, as well as for children, e.g. The Jungle Book in 1894.

In 1892 Arthur Conan Doyle brought the detective story to a new height with The Adventures of Sherlock Holmes. H. G. Wells wrote his first science fiction stories in the 1880s. One of his best known is "The Country of the Blind" in 1904.

In the United States, Herman Melville published his story collection The Piazza Tales in 1856. "The Celebrated Jumping Frog of Calaveras County" was the title story of Mark Twain's first book one year later.

In 1884, Brander Matthews, the first American professor of dramatic literature, published "The Philosophy of the Short-Story".

During that same year, Matthews was the first writer to name the emerging genre "short story". Another theorist of narrative fiction was Henry James. James wrote a lot of short stories himself, including "The Real Thing" in 1892, "Maud-Evelyn" and The Beast in the Jungle in1903.

In the 1890s Kate Chopin published short stories in several magazines.

The most prolific French author of short stories was Guy de Maupassant. With his stories like "Boule de Suif", "Ball of Fat" in 1880 and "L'Inutile Beauté", "The Useless Beauty", in 1890 are just great examples of French realism.

In Russia

Ivan Sergeyevitch Turgenev was born in the city of Oryol, central Russia, on October 28, 1818, and died in France on September 3, 1883, with Madame Viardot and their children by his side.

He spent most of his childhood on the family estate under the instruction of tutors until he enrolled at the University of Moscow in 1833. A year had passed, he transferred to the University of Petersburg, from which he graduated in 1837.

Turgenev traveled for some time in Europe, especially Germany, and chiefly studied philosophy. In 1843, he accepted a minor post in the Ministry of the Interior and made the acquaintance of Pauline Viardot, a sophisticated French singer whom he remained devoted to for the rest of his life. Sometimes, he would often remain abroad for long periods of time.

Ivan Turgenev gained recognition with his story collection "A Sportsman's Sketches".

Nikolai Semyonovich Leskov

Born 4 February 1831 – Died 21 February 1895

He was a Russian novelist, short-story writer, playwright, and journalist, who also wrote under the pseudonym M. Stebnitsky.

He was praised for his unique writing style and innovative experiments in form, and held in high esteem by Leo Tolstoy, Anton Chekhov and Maxim Gorky among others, Leskov is credited with creating a comprehensive picture of contemporary Russian society using mostly short literary forms.

His major work included Lady Macbeth of Mtsensk in 1865. Later, it was made into an opera by Shostakovich.

More of his work:

"The Cathedral Clergy" in 1872

"The Enchanted Wanderer" in 1873

"The Tale of Cross-eyed Lefty from Tula" in 1881

"The Steel Flea "in 1881

In India

Rabindranath Tagore published short stories. It was on the lives of the poor and oppressed such as peasants, women and villagers under colonial misrule and exploitation.

In Poland

Bolesław Prus was the most important author of short stories. In 1888 he wrote "A Legend of Old Egypt".

In Brazil

Machado de Assis, Joaquim Maria 1839-1908

He was one of the major's novelists from Brazil. Machado was the most important short story writer from his country at the time, under the influences, among others, of Xavier de Maistre, Lawrence Sterne, Guy de Maupassant.

Lima Barreto

Born Afonso Henriques de Lima Barreto

13 May 1881
Rio de Janeiro, Empire of Brazil
Died 1 November 1922 at the age of 41
Rio de Janeiro, Brazil
Occupation-Novelist, short story writer, journalist
Nationality-Brazilian
Literary movement- Pre-Modernism
Notable works - Triste Fim de Policarpo Quaresma,
Os Bruzundangas, Clara dos Anjos, O Cemitério dos Vivos
Relatives Afonso Celso de Assis Figueredo

At the end of the 19th century, the writer, Lima Barreto became popular with short stories about bohemianism. His writing is about the former slaves, and very ironical about nationalism. Lima Barreto died almost forgotten, however, he became very popular in the 20th century.

In Portuguese literature, the major names of the time are Almeida Garrett and the historian and novelist Alexandre Herculano. Still influential, Eça de Queiroz produced some short stories with a style influenced by Émile Zola, Balzac, and Dickens.

STORY DURING 1900–1945

In the United Kingdom, periodicals like The Strand Magazine and Storyteller contributed to the popularity of the short story. Hector Hugh Munro,1870–1916, also known by his pen name of Saki, wrote satirical short stories about Edwardian England.

W. Somerset Maugham, who wrote over a hundred short stories, was one of the most popular authors of his time.

P. G. Wodehouse published his first collection of comical stories about valet Jeeves in 1917.

Many detective stories were written by G. K. Chesterton, Agatha Christie, and Dorothy L. Sayers.

Short stories by Virginia Woolf are "Kew Gardens" in 1919 and "Solid Objects," about a politician with mental problems.

Graham Greene wrote his Twenty-One Stories between 1929 and 1954.

A specialist of the short story was V. S. Pritchett, whose first collection appeared in 1932.

Arthur C. Clarke published his first science fiction story, "Travel by Wire!" in 1937. Evelyn Waugh, Muriel Spark, and L. P. Hartley were other popular British storytellers whose career started in this period.

In Ireland, James Joyce published his short story collection Dubliners in 1914. These stories, written in a more accessible style than his later novels, are based on careful observation of the inhabitants of his birth city.

During the first half of the 20th century, several high-profile American magazines such as The Atlantic Monthly, Harper's Magazine, The New Yorker, Scribner's, The Saturday Evening Post, Esquire, and The Bookman published short stories in each issue.

The demand for quality short stories was great. The money was so great that F. Scott Fitzgerald repeatedly turned to short stories. Writing helped him to pay his numerous debts. His first collection Flappers and Philosophers appeared in book form in 1920.

William Faulkner wrote over one hundred short stories. Go Down, Moses, a collection of seven stories, appeared in 1941.

Ernest Hemingway's concise writing style was perfectly fit for shorter fiction. Stories like "A Clean, Well-Lighted Place" in 1926, "Hills Like White Elephants" in 1927 and "The Snows of Kilimanjaro" in 1936 are only a few pages long, but carefully crafted.

Dorothy Parker's bittersweet story "Big Blonde" debuted in 1929. A popular science fiction story is "Nightfall" by Isaac Asimov.

Katherine Mansfield from New Zealand wrote many short stories between 1912 until her death in 1923. "The Doll's House" in 1922 treats the topic of social inequity.

Two important authors of short stories in the German language were Thomas Mann and Franz Kafka. In 1922 the latter wrote "A Hunger Artist", about a man who fasts for several days.

In Japan

Ryūnosuke Akutagawa,1892–1927, is called the Father of the Japanese short story.

In Brazil, the most famous modern short story writer is Mário de Andrade. At the time, Paulistan writer António de Alcantâra Machado became very popular from his collection of short stories titled, Brás, Bexiga e Barra Funda in 192. Some of his stories are read around several Italian neighborhoods, but now he is mostly read in just São Paulo. Also, novelist Graciliano Ramos and poet Carlos Drummond de Andrade have significant short story works.

Portuguese writers like Mário de Sá-Carneiro, Florbela Espanca and Fernando Pessoa wrote well-known short stories, although their major genre was poetry.

The period following World War II saw a great flowering of literary short fiction in the United States. The New Yorker continued to publish the works of the form's leading mid-century practitioners, including

Shirley Jackson, whose story, "The Lottery", was published in 1948. It caused the strongest response in the magazine's history of that era.

There were other frequent contributors during the last 1940s which included John Cheever, John Steinbeck, Jean Stafford, and Eudora Welty.

J. D. Salinger's Nine Stories, in 1953, experimented with point of view and voice, while Flannery O'Connor's story "A Good Man is Hard to Find", in 1955, revived the Southern Gothic style.

Cultural and social identity played a considerable role in much of the short fiction of the 1960s. Philip Roth and Grace Paley cultivated distinctive Jewish-American voices.

Tillie Olsen's "I Stand Here Ironing", in 1961, adopted a consciously feminist perspective.

James Baldwin's collection Going to Meet the Man, 1965, told stories of African American life.

Frank O'Connor's '' The Lonely Voice", an exploration of the short story, appeared in 1963.

Wallace Stenger's short stories are primarily set in the American West.

Stephen King published many short stories in men's magazines in the 1960s and after.

The 1970s saw the rise of the postmodern short story in the works of Donald Barthelme and John Barth.

Traditional writers included John Updike and Joyce Carol Oates. They maintained significant influence on the form of short stories.

Simplicity gained widespread influence in the 1980s. It most notably in the work of Raymond Carver and Ann Beattie.

Canadian short story writers include Alice Munro, Mavis Gallant, and Lynn Coady.

In the United Kingdom, Daphne du Maurier wrote suspense stories like "The Birds" in 1952 and "Don't Look Now" in 1971.

Roald Dahl was the master of the twist-in-the-tale. Short story collections like "Lamb to the Slaughter" in 1953 and "Kiss Kiss" in 1960 illustrated his dark humor.

In Italy, Italo Calvino published the short story collection Marco Valdo, about a poor man in a city, in 1963.

In Brazil, the short story became popular among female writers such as Clarice Inspector, Lygia Fagundes Telles, Adélia Prado, who wrote about their society from a feminine viewpoint.

There were also male writers, like Dalton Trevisan, Autran Dourado Moacyr Scliar and Carlos Heitor Cony that wrote about the same cause of that time.

Also, writing about poverty and the favelas, João Antonio became a well-known writer. Other post-modern short fiction authors included writers like Hilda Hilst and Caio Fernando Abreu.

Detective literature was led by Ruben Fonseca. It is also necessary to mention João Guimarães Rosa, who wrote short stories in the book Sagarana using a complex, experimental language based on tales of oral tradition.

Portuguese writers like Virgílo Ferreira, Fernando Goncalves Namora and Sophia de Mello Breyner Andresen are among the most influential short story writers from 20th-century Portuguese language literature.

Manuel da Silva Ramos is one of the most well-known names of postmodernism in the country. Nobel Prize-winner José Saramago published a few short stories but became popular from his novels.

The Angolan writer José Luandino Vieira is one of the most well-known writers from his country and has several short stories. José Eduardo Agualusa is also increasingly read in Portuguese-speaking countries.

Mozambican Mia Couto is a widely known writer of postmodern prose, and he is read even in non-Portuguese speaking countries. Other Mozambican writers such as Suleiman Cassamo, Paulina Chiziane and Eduardo White are gaining popularity with Portuguese-speakers too.

The Argentine writer Jorge Luis Borges is one of the most famous writers of short stories in the Spanish language. "The Library of Babel" in 1941 and "The Aleph" in 1945 handle difficult subjects like infinity. Two of the most representative writers of the Magical realism genre are also widely known Argentinian short story writers: Adolfo Bioy Casares and Julio Cortázar.

The Uruguayan writer Juan Carlos Onetti is known as one of the most important magical realist writers from Latin America.

In Colombia, the Nobel prize laureate author Gabriel Garcia Marquez is the main novelist and short story writer, known by his magical realist stories and his defense of the Communist Party in his country.

The Peruvian writer Mario Vargas Llosa, also a Nobel prize winner, has significant short story works.

The Egyptian Nobel Prize-winner Naguib Mafouz is the most well-known author from his country but has only a few short stories.

Japanese world-known short story writers include Kenzaburō Ōe Nobel prize winner of 1994, Yukio Mishima and Haruki Murakami.

Multi-awarded Philippine writer Peter Solis Nery is one of the most famous writers of short stories in Hiligaynon language. His stories "Lirio" in 1998, "Candido" in 2007, "Donato Bugtot" in 2011, and "Si Padre Olan kag ang Dios" in 2013 are all gold prize winners at the Palanca Awards of Philippine Literature.

<u>ELEMENTS OF A SHORT STORY</u>

A character, sometimes known as a fictional character, is a person or other being in a narrative work of art such as a novel, play, television series, film, or video game the character may be entirely fictional or based on a real-life person, in which case the distinction of a "fictional" versus "real" character may be made.

Derived from the ancient Greek word χαρακτήρ, the English word dates from the Restoration, although it became widely used after its appearance in Tom Jones in 1749.

From this, the sense of "a part played by an actor" developed. Character, particularly when acted by an actor in the theatre or cinema, involves "the illusion of being a human person."

In literature, characters guide readers through their stories, helping them to understand plots and ponder themes.

Since the end of the 18th century, the phrase "in character" has been used to describe an effective impersonation by an actor.

Since the 19th century, the art of creating characters, as practiced by actors or writers, has been called characterization.

A character who stands as a representative of a particular class or group of people is known as a type. Types include both stock characters and those that are more fully individualized.

The characters in Henrik Ibsen's Hedda Gabler in 1891 and August Strindberg's Miss Julie in 1888, for example, are representative of specific positions in the social relations of class and gender, such that the conflicts between the characters reveal ideological conflicts.

The study of a character requires an analysis of its relations with all the other characters in the work the individual status of a character is defined through the network of oppositions proairetic, pragmatic, linguistic, proxemic that it forms with the other characters.

The relation between characters and the action of the story shifts historically, often miming shifts in society and its ideas about human individuality, self-determination, and social order.

Antagonist Antihero Archenemy Character Arc Characterization Deuteragonist False Protagonist Focal Character Foil Protagonist Stock Character Supporting character Tritagonist Narrator Tragic hero.

The PLOT

The Plot refers to the sequence of events inside a story which affect other events through the principle of cause and effect. The causal events of a plot can be thought of as a series of sentences linked by "and so". Plots can vary from simple structures such as in a traditional ballad to complex interwoven structures sometimes referred to as an imbroglio. The term plot can serve as a verb and refer to a character planning future actions in the story.

In the narrative sense, the term highlights the important points which have important consequences within the story, according to Ansen Dibell. The term is similar in meaning to the term storyline.

Action Backstory Cliché Climax Cliffhanger Conflict Deus ex Machina Dialogue Dramatic Structure Exposition Eucatastrophe Foreshadowing Flashback Flashforward Frame Story In medias res Pace Plot Device Plot Twist Poetic Justice Reveal Self-fulfilling Prophecy Subplot Trope Kishōtenketsu.

The setting

The setting is both the time and geographic location within a narrative or within a work of fiction. A literary element, the setting helps initiate the main backdrop and mood for a story. Setting has been referred to as story world [1] or milieu to include a context, especially society, beyond the immediate surroundings of the story. Elements of setting may include culture, historical period, geography, and hour. Along with the plot, character, theme, and style, setting is considered one of the fundamental components of fiction.

The Theme

In contemporary literary studies, a theme is the central topic a text treats. Themes can be divided into two categories: a work's thematic concept is what readers "think the work is about" and its thematic statement being "what the work says about the subject".

The most common contemporary understanding of theme is an idea or point that is central to a story, which can often be summed in a single word e.g., love, death, betrayal.

Typical examples of themes of this type are conflict between the individual and society; coming of age; humans in conflict with technology; nostalgia; and the dangers of unchecked ambition.

A theme may be exemplified by the actions, utterances, or thoughts of a character in a novel. An example of this would be the thematic idea of loneliness in John Steinbeck's of Mice and Men, wherein many of the characters seem to be lonely. It may differ from the thesis—the text's or author's implied worldview.

A story may have several themes. Themes often explore historically common or cross-culturally recognizable ideas, such as ethical questions, and are usually implied rather than stated explicitly. An example of this would be whether one should live a seemingly better life, at the price of giving up parts of one's humanity, which is a theme in Aldous Huxley's Brave New World. Along with plot, character, setting, and style, theme is considered one of the components of fiction

The Style

In literature, writing style is the manner of expressing thought in language characteristic of an individual, period, school, or nation. Beyond the essential elements of spelling, grammar, and punctuation, writing style is the choice of words, sentence structure, and paragraph structure, used to convey the meaning effectively.

The former is referred to as rules, elements, essentials, mechanics, or handbook; the latter are referred to as style, or rhetoric. The rules are about what a writer does; style is about how the writer does it.

While following the rules drawn from established English usage, a writer has great flexibility in how to express a concept. The point of good writing style is to express the message to the reader simply, clearly, and convincingly; always keep the reader attentive, engaged, and interested.

Never display the writer's personality. What I am trying to say is the author must demonstrate writer's skills, knowledge, or abilities. Those qualities are usually evident and are what experts consider the writer's individual style.

The Structure

The setup, act one, is where all the main characters and their basic situations are introduced. The first act contains the primary level of characterization. That is where it is exploring the character's backgrounds and personalities. A problem is also introduced, which is what drives the story forward.

The second act, the conflict, is the bulk of the story, and begins when the inciting incident or catalyst sets things into motion.

This is the part of the story where the characters go through major changes in their lives because of what is happening; this can be referred to as the character arc, or character development.

The third act, or resolution, is when the problem in the story boils over, forcing the characters to confront it, allowing all the elements of the story to come together and inevitably leading to the ending.

Gathering My Work

I began stacking up my inventory of stories on my desk and read them. I experimented with each selection.

I was so surprised by the different events I have written. There were many stories I had forgotten.

I had lots of choices. I added pieces to my collection and removed some. I realized some needed more work. Some were stronger than others.

I chose stories that seemed to fit together, give variety, and reflected the book's themes. The themes emerged as I worked on the book. I saw how my fiction had changed over time, saw the obsessions that haunted me as a writer. I had written again and again about relationships, bonds to partners, spouses, parents, children, and friends, as if I were trying to find a solution to a puzzle, to understand those things that strengthen or weaken relationships.

I didn't include a few of my favorite stories in the collection. They didn't touch on the book's themes or dealt with ideas explored in other pieces. Still, it was hard to part with them.

I tried to really consider each piece…

When I started to write, my goal was to create a story that worked. This can take years. It did for me. Each story was a journey into the unknown. I work over a story, examining descriptions, words, images, and character development, trying to make a piece work.

A writer is never really done with a project, even though he or she moves on to the next one. I had considered many of my stories finished, especially the published ones. I ended up revising the stories that were part of the collection.

I was flexible….

After setting the story collection, I put the manuscript aside. I kept writing new ones. I then considered the stronger one.

The collection was on its way….

I always consider the Arrangement of each story.

I re checked the order of the stories. In a sense, a reader participates in the order; he or she can choose to read the stories in any order. Still, I felt the arrangement was important and created a flow for the book.

Who doesn't love a short love story?

Since the start of human storytelling history, humans have enjoyed great romance stories. Everybody wants to feel some of that romance and reading very short romantic stories is often a great way to quench that thirst.

I've compiled several love stories for you to read. All the stories are very short and can bring some of that romantic spark into your life. These are great reads whether you're celebrating Valentine's Day or just itching for a romantic spark.

The following are stories that will make you smile or even bring back beautiful memories of yesteryears….

I hope you enjoy reading my work because it was written just for you….

Contents

Chapter 1

My First Love

I was just sixteen when I fell in love with George. It was the most thrilling feeling. I still cannot get over it, as they say when a woman falls in love, she can never fall in love again.

Although I was a teenager then, I still have vivid memories of that young man and how I felt for him.

I was a smart, bubbly, and cute little teenager, who enjoyed life. I was living life to the fullest. Life changed for me the minute I set my eyes on George.

It all began on the first day of school back in 1964. We were in the 9th grade. The teacher was going on and on about classroom rules.

George was talking with his friends about the summer vacation. I found him so handsome, his curly, dark brown hair and large dark brown eyes were just perfect! I was stunned!

Though now when I look back, I laugh it off as mere infatuation, but I don't know why I felt an instant connection with him. I guess the summer vacation made a change in all of us. I have known George since the 4th grade. This is the first time I found him so handsome.

Every time he looked into my eyes; my body trembled. I used to feel so nervous and excited at the same time.

You won't believe it, but we never really had a conversation. We just knew each other from school. Still, I felt a strong connection with this guy. All I remember was that he was so handsome and so good-looking.

Whenever I used to look at him, I could not stop myself from staring at him. He never bothered to even turn around to look at me. To him, I was insignificant as I was much younger than him. He didn't even try to take any interest in me.

Each day when I used to go to school, I used to fix my hair differently and wear my best of dresses to look nice. I just wanted him to notice me. He used to be so occupied in chatting and playing with his friends that he hardly took notice of me.

I was so angry at him that I used to stand in the hallway for hours waiting. I just wanted to get a glimpse of him. Sometimes I used to keep peeping out of the window of our classroom.

I wanted to see him play in the school yard. I would spot him only a few times. The rest of the time I would just sadly retreat to my studies or start helping the teacher with some other work.

As days passed, things remained the same. Then slowly and gradually he started noticing that I was staring at him. When I am around him, in school or in the school yard, he starts looking at me.

Once I remember I was standing in the neighborhood bakery and he suddenly walked in with his friends, probably to buy something. I turned around and as usual started staring at him. He was standing opposite me when suddenly a lot of people came in between us. It was a funny situation, and I could see just one half of his face and I caught him staring at me with one eye!

I was shocked as it was so sudden and the depth with which he was staring at me cannot be explained in words. There was admiration and tender love in them! I then left the bakery feeling very happy and still now I cannot forget that look of his in the bakery.

Another time I felt very nervous was when we both passed each other coming back from school. I was walking on the side of the road, and he suddenly saw me. I was swaying my school bag along my side.

He was walking with his friend and when I passed him, I stopped swaying my bag. I quietly tried to pass him and then he turned around and looked fondly at me! I walked away feeling cautious and embarrassed at the same time.

Every time I came in direct contact with George and whenever he looked at me, I always felt a soft tenderness in his eyes. There was warm in his heart that touched me deep inside.

George was very tall and fair. He had beautiful hair and a very nice moustache. Whenever I looked at him, my knees got weak. I used to dream of him being near me and talking to me.

I also imagine that we spent time with each other. I could never get enough courage to ever stand in front of him and talk. I was too young and too naive to even think of it!

Things went on in this way for a few months and nothing happened. Until one fine day he smiled at me! Just imagine my prince charming smiled at me. Finally, he noticed me. I must tell you; it was the most beautiful smile I had ever seen!

I was coming back from school one evening. George was sitting on his bike waiting for his friends. He saw me coming. I passed him and he did not say anything, but when I went a little further and turned around, I saw George smiling at me. I was shocked.

I finally went home without talking to my prince. I did not know what to do, but I was fascinated by his first smile. It was so sudden that I was at a loss for words. I didn't know what to do

Fate had other plans for me. Just imagine my bad luck, that when I could think of having a relationship with George, as he had finally acknowledged my presence and smiled at me, I had to go, I had to leave the city for good!

My father was relocated to another town, and I had to leave the very next day! I had to travel all alone, as my dad had arranged for me to attend another school in that new town. I had to leave. I could have had a beautiful relationship with George.

I still don't know whether it was love at first sight with him or was its infatuation, but one thing I must say and that it was love. I will never forget him ever and all that I felt for him.

Certainly, it was my first love, whether it was infatuation or not I don't know, but it was my first experience of any exposure to the opposite sex, and you won't believe it that I could never like any other person ever in my life after that, other than my husband!

First love is like a fresh blooming flower in the morning sunlight. It is like the first most memorable fragrance you might have smelt in your entire life! It is the most wonderful feeling anyone can ever have.

Those of you who are reading this story, might feel that I am crazy as I am calling my first crush to be my first love, but only I know how I felt when I was around him and when he looked into my eyes, it was the most ultimate feeling I have ever had in my life. It is unforgettable and I still cherish those tender feelings I had for him!

All of those who have such first loves or crushes as mine will very well understand what I am talking about. When their love does not reach any culmination then they will also feel the same way that I am feeling. Whenever I feel very lonely and lost, I think of George. I ask God that why he did not unite me with him, why am I subjected to such misery of losing my love at such a tender age.

I am happy in my present life but when I think of George, I cannot calm myself.

Anyways those are ways of God. No one can question them, but again I want to repeat that was my first love and I will never forget it ever.

Chapter 2

The Car Crash

Every day at about 7 a.m., Sofia takes her daughter to school. This morning was no different…

Sandy was fourteen years old. She was very popular in school. Sometimes that drove Sofia crazy because she had to take her daughter from one school activity to the next.

Half of the time Sofia was a walking zombie. Taking care of a house and working in her own flower shop was no joke. You see, Sandy's father was killed in Irak, therefore, Sofia was a single parent.

When Sofia was driving Sandy to school, she was a witness to a shocking car crash. The accident was serious, so she got out of her car to see if she could help.

There were two cars involved in the accident. One of the cars, an SUV, quickly started to catch fire. She immediately checked if there were passengers left in the car.

Sofia saw an unconscious fourteen-year-old boy. Without hesitating, she pulled the car door open and brought the boy to safety. He was brought to a hospital where Sofia and her daughter visited him several times to help him recover.

As time started to pass by, Sofia noticed that her daughter started to go to the hospital on her own account. As it turns out, the two teens were falling in love with each other.

Sandy told her mother that she started liking Kevin the minute he was admitted in the hospital. Sandy recognized Kevin right away. They were in the same school and took some classes together. Sandy really helps Kevin recover faster than expected.

Unfortunately, both Kevin parent died after a week in the hospital. Kevin was left in his aunt's care. He wasn't told about that until he was fully recovered.

Every afternoon, right after school, Sandy would visit Kevin and put him update with schoolwork.

Kevin had a happy life with his aunt and cousin. He graduated from high school and got a scholarship to Harvard University. Sofia also received a scholarship, and both enter Harvard in the year2010.

They graduated from Harvard University and became lawyers. They opened a law firm in the state of New York.

I forgot to inform you that they got married and had a set of twins….

Chapter 3

A Teen on the Run

When a young student of a Catholic Church asked her teacher about the reasons why she decided to become a religious sister, her teacher told her a heartwarming love story.

Many years ago, when she was at a similar age, the teacher, Ms. Patterson, fell in love with a young man stemming from a wealthy family.

The two began seeing each other and quickly developed a deep connection with each other.

Unfortunately, the young man's family was not at all in agreement with the relationship.

They even threatened to enroll their son at a university overseas and far away. As Ms. Patterson came from a poor background, she couldn't possibly have afforded to go with him at that time.

This meant that if they wanted to continue the relationship, they would be separated from each other whether they wanted it or not.

But they both had fallen so in love with each other that ending the relationship, no matter in what way, was not an option.

For this reason, they decided to run away. In great secrecy, they planned their escape and set these plans into action when the young man's family finally found out about it.

But instead of quickly returning home after running away, the two never went back. They joined the church, took holy orders, and began traveling the world for various humanitarian missions.

The two spent 40 years traveling and even got married, shortly before the man's life came to an end.

Chapter 4

The Surgery

Monica was a beautiful little girl that needed a heart operation. She came from a very poor family; therefore, it was hard to get the money right away.

All the neighbors and classmates made collections throughout a small village in South America.

When a surgeon operated on Monica, complications started to arise. She lost a lot of blood and needed a blood transfusion.

However, she had blood type O, which wasn't available in the hospital.

The surgeon, therefore, asked the girl's little brother, who was an O-type as well, if they could draw blood from him. He explained that it was incredibly important.

It was a matter of life and death. The young boy, seemingly afraid, sat a couple of moments in silence until he finally agreed.

He got up and hugged his parents, wishing them goodbye. After the nurses had taken the blood from him, he whispered anxiously to ask if they knew how many minutes he had left to live.

He was absolutely convinced that he was going to die so that his sister could live. And he was willing to do so.

When the nurses realized that the young boy thought he was going to die, they cheered him up and explained to him that he had many wonderful and joyful decades left to live.

Chapter 5

A Loving Father

Carmela thought that she had the perfect family. Since she was a young girl, her parents always gave her everything she needed and even much more....

One day Carmela found a worn-down diary in a toolbox that belonged to her dad. It was his diary. He wrote it about the time he was only 16 years old.

Carmela unconditionally loves her dad, who is not only the best dad but also a loving and kind husband. It wasn't easy for her to open the diary, but eventually, she became so curious about his life that she decided to read it.

The last entry in the diary was a short paragraph, wildly scribbled down. It said that at the time of writing the entry, that he was 16 years old and an alcoholic.

He went on describing that he dropped out from high school with a criminal record. Her dad also noted in the entry that one month later he would become a teen father.

At that point, Carmela began to cry. She was crying because her father became a changed man when he found out that he was going to be a father. In those notes, he also made the promised to himself that he would set his life straight. He would become the father for his little daughter that he never had...

Chapter 6

Pepito

Mr. Rios and his wife were very happy to move from a big city to the quiet life in the country. The people there were very humble and caring.

Esther was happy and at other times, very sad. She was happy when she was around people.

The minute they left their house or a gathering a sad feeling dominated her body and soul.

Mr. Rios was different because he had his books and all his friends in the library.

One day, Esther told her husband she wanted a bird or dog. Mr. Rios didn't like animals. He told her that she can buy herself a bird....

Esther got up the next day very happy. She headed to a pet shop not too far from their house.

While looking for the best bird, she notices a tiny African grey parrot. The bird was only a couple of days old. Esther never had a bird; however, she was sure this was the right one.

She bought all the necessary accessories for the bird. It was a very huge cage. The store owner explained that the bird was going to grow fast. And guess what? It sure did.

Esther taught him how to sing. That bird imitated her all the time. Sometimes Mr. Rios didn't know if the bird was talking or the wife.

He hated that bird because it never kept quiet. Esther, in the other hand, was a happy trooper.

Esther decided to name the bird Pepito. She likes the sound of it. Many years went by and Mr. Rios and Pepito never became friends. Pepito only had one owner and that was Esther.

Pepito was so smart that he knew when Esther was sick. Esther had lung cancer and didn't want her husband to know about it. She was always caring for the bird that Mr. Rios never notice any changed in his wife's behavior.

One morning, Mr. Rios got up to make breakfast. He noticed that his wife didn't move. He got closer to the bed and found out that his wife has died in her sleep.

Mr. Rios was very sad. He was walking around just like a robot. He didn't want to go to the library or meet with his groups.

It took months for Mr. Rios slowly get back to reality......

Mr. Rios tried very hard to be Pepito's friend. Pepito didn't care about Mr. Rios. Pepito got fed but that was it. There was no bond of any kind between man and bird....

Mr. Rios started a new routine after Esther died....

Mr. Rios liked to start his day in the library. It was a brief walk from his home. It was conveniently situated at the top of the main street near the market. That was the house that he and his wife had retired to.

When they first moved, he join the local writing group which met at the library. He would spend many happy, creative hours in its welcoming embrace.

He told his wife that it was as much group therapy as creative writing. Sadly, it was all gone now. People had moved away, lost interest, or died. He was the only one left of the old crowd.

He and the chief librarian, Mrs. Prado, who was approaching retirement. Mrs. Padro had a soft spot for Mr. Rios. She had known his wife, Esther. She enjoyed talking to him.

Mr. Rios was like a permanent fixture at the library. He always sat in his corner, reading the newspaper.

Mr. Rios finished reading the paper and searched around preparing to leave. He checked that he hadn't left anything: gloves, hat, scarf, phone, then walked across the street to "Mama's Café" for his morning coffee. It was the only pleasure he had in life but a real pleasure indeed.

He arrived home at about noon, unlocked the door and stepped into the hall.

"Hello," called a cheerful voice, that sounded very much like his own. It was Pepito, an African grey parrot. He moved it from the lounge to the hall because of its constant interruptions to his television programs.

It had been Esther's idea to buy one, and now she was gone. He really wanted no part of that bird, but he was stuck with it.

"Hello," said the parrot again.

"Get lost," was what Mr. Rios wanted to say, but he could imagine the expected effects if he did. He ignored the parrot and walked through to the kitchen, to make himself a sandwich. He coughed several times. The parrot coughed back.

"Hello," it called. "Would you like a cup of tea?" Mr. Rios came back from the kitchen holding a packet of seeds and filled up the parrot's feeder. "Hello," it said again, Mr. Rios sighed.

Mr. Rios was thinking about the little job he had planned for the afternoon. He heard scratching noises in the attic last night. It was October and he guessed that the mice had left their summer quarters in the garden.

Now, they were making themselves comfortable in the attic. They were getting ready for the winter.

The noises had come from above his bedroom at the back of the cottage. He changed into a pair of overalls, put on a disposable dust mask, and recovered the bar that released the attic hatch from the hook on the wall of his utility room.

"That's the ticket my friend," said the parrot. Mr. Rios lifted the metal bar in his hands as he walked past the bird.

"Hello," it said.

Mr. Rios opened the hatch and let the ladder down. He climbed up into the attic carrying his traps and a small quantity of peanut butter in an empty margarine box: he had read that mice preferred it to cheese. He heard the parrot calling from below, "That's the ticket my friend."

It was very in the attic; it had been a hot day. He stepped carefully across to where the beams inclined down and joined with the ceiling beams.

He then knelt and crawled into a narrow space. He lay down sweating on the floor. He then began to lay his traps, pushing them into the attic.

Mr. Rios was beginning to feel weak. The heat in the attic was taking over. It was then that the heart attack struck. His chest cramped. It felt as if it was being crushed by an enormous crab's claw.

He lay back breathless. Mr. Rios tried so hard to call for help, however, there was no one around only his crazy bird.

"What's the time?" called the parrot.

Mr. Rios fell into a place between sleeping and waking, heat and cold, and called for help when he had the strength.

Mrs. Padro walked by Mr. Rios' house on her way home from the library. She hadn't seen him for two days. She decided to visit him. She wanted to see if he was alright.

Mrs. Prado walked up the path and knocked on the door.

"Hello," called a voice.

"Hello," she called back, "Are you alright, Mr. Rios?" she heard coughing.

"Help me," called Mr. Rios from the attic but his voice was too weak. Mrs. Prado didn't hear him. The parrot cocked its head. All she could hear was that crazy bird….

"What's the time?" it called.

"About five," called the librarian. The parrot coughed again. "Are you sure you're alright? I'm on my way home, do you need anything?"

"Would you like a cup of tea?" asked the parrot.

"Help me," called Mr. Rios faintly…

"No thanks, I'm on my way home, George will be expecting me."

"That's the ticket my friend," said the parrot.

Mrs. Prado walked back up the front path and went home.

Two more days passed and by this time Mr. Rios was dead. He lay rigid and drying in the heat of the attic. Mrs. Prado knocked at the door of the cottage.

"Hello," she called.

"Hello," said a voice.

"Are you alright, Mr. Rios? You're not coughing as much, you sound better."

"That's the ticket my friend"

She shrugged and continued her way home.

Another two days passed, and Mrs. Prado knocked again, "Hello."

The parrot, standing on its perch, looked at its empty water bottle and empty feeder. It raised a leg, cocked its head on one side and began to scratch it.

"Help me,' it called loudly, "help me."

Chapter 7

The Lonely Immigrant

Tomas Nevarez, that's my name. A name that had been announced all over the world. I had won the Lottery; the publicity stunt that had become a periodic tradition.

I didn't intend on winning so much money. I got the ticket because my girlfriend was making a big deal about it. She said that I was going to win big time. I just laughed. It seemed to make her happy that I bought it.

The thing is I didn't consider myself lucky to be getting an "all expenses" paid trip for an "out of this world adventure." I won, and that was a billion to one odd that would happen.

Now I'm going, now I'm the middle class nobody who gets to go to California. I will be famous for as long as I was up there with the rich famous. I'd be forgotten the moment we touch bottom.

Reality is that the real millionare would have lots of real important data to share with the world. All I could say was how weird it is to be with the rich and being noticed for a while.

I was acting as enthusiastic as I could. Only I hadn't paid much attention to the well displayed information on trips and interviews. I was to attend many gatherings.

This wasn't a run-of-the-park. Nor was it a quick run to the store. It was to be the fifteenth day away from my friends and family. My destination was to conquer the world.

Not just any place, it was California. This trip was 'special.' It was a state just about the size of two or three towns put together. A little larger in fact.

I we able to walk around town easily. What wouldn't be easy would be talking to people. I had no knowledge of the English language. Yeah, it was that kind of place where they looked down at Hispanics.

They didn't want their town to go down in price. Those racist had no idea of how smart we are.

As I started walking towards a coffee shop, a patrol car stopped me and asked me for my papers. I had no idea what those papers were. I only had the key to my room. The officers got annoyed with me and pushed me into the patrol car.

That was the first time I felt so lonely in my life. Back home, I had so many friends. Here in California, we were called the immigrants. I tried to tell the police that I had won the lottery. The whole precinct laughed at me. I wasn't doing well all with my poor English.

A couple of hours went by. No one came for me. The cops didn't even give me food or anything to drink. They decided to turn the TV on. The news was about to begin. They were all surprised to see my face on TV.

The reporters were just giving information about me! Even the major and a whole staff from the country came to the TV station. They stated that I was a very important citizen and if anyone knew my whereabouts to please contact the hotel or the media.

Slowly, the cops turned to me. They tried to be nice, but it was too late. I got a translator that explained how much money I won. I was going to present a City in California with a large amount of money.

Now, I decided to go to another state where the treaty everyone equally. My fiancé flew down to New York to meet me. I went to Spanish Harlem and gave money to all the Hispanics that were living in real bad housing.

The New York City Major thank me and informed me that I had plenty of relatives and friends in New York. I couldn't believe my eyes when I saw my fiancé and all those lost relatives that moved to the city that never sleep for a better life.

I am proud to report to everyone that I was given a medal for helping the poor. The police, firemen, and doctors were present at that press conference. I told the press that I wanted to see students and teachers there.

Why I was asked, because they are the future. We must tell the young ones to respect everyone no matter what their nationality or income was.

The reporters asked me, "what were my plans now that I was in New York?" I smiled and told them that the first thing I was going to do was go back to school and learn English.

I then told everyone that I was going to marry the love of my life, Maria. With Maria at my side, I knew that I wasn't lonely anymore.

We had a lovely wedding in Central Park. The invitation was for the rich as well as the poor.

Chapter 8

A Strange Love Story

Carmela's breathing was deep and steady. She was running through the dense forest holding her mother's kitchen knife in her hand.

Her dress was torn up, also her legs, hands and her face were cut by the tree branches.

"Stop you are the victim", said the forest while burying its thorns in her.

"Stop and wait for the big brave man to save you", shouted the animals in the forest.

"Go back to being the naïve little girl", the strangers whispered with an outrageous mumble.

It was wrong, she knew it, they knew it even her lover knew it.

That is the only way you can go on with life is to marry Kevin. He is a smart man. "Don't go ruining it for all of us," her family warned her.

You need to wait for us to save you, said her parents. with a commanding voice.

You don't have the right to change anything in life, her grandmother waves her finger in front of her face.

You are wearing red; you know what it means, right? Blamed her new boyfriend. He is the one that brought the wine in the nearby liquor store. You asked for it, stop complaining and carry on with your part of the deal.

Carmela listens, for so many years and for so many times, that this story was told.

She didn't want to disappoint her family or make them mad, angry or sad.

Not anymore…

She did her part in the plan made for her. She played cards right.

Arturo was not far away from her. She could see him running after her. He was panicking and hysterical. His breathing was short and fast. A white foam was accumulating around his mouth. His big, impressive eyes were now nothing but sheer horror.

She was faster than him, stronger than he had ever been.

She was the predator he was the prey.

"Can you hear me know with your big ears?" She screamed.

"Can you see me with your big blue eyes?" She roars as a lioness.

He falls exhausted, nothing was left of him. She looked at him, he was weak and pathetic.

Around them the forest was quiet, nothing and nobody asked her to stop anymore.

They all knew. The truth….

Chapter 9

Just One Call

One night on my way home, I made eye contact with a gorgeous young woman. I went back to my phone and didn't think much of it, but she came and sat next to me.

I got very nervous. I didn't say anything. After several stops, she asked if the bus was going to a certain stop. I gave her a quick, 'Yeah, the sign is over there,' trying to avoid being the creepy passenger that's more interested in the person than providing directions.

She was persistent and kept asking too many questions. I gave her my business card before I got off the bus.

Lydia pointed out that my cell phone number wasn't on it. I laughed and told her that it was a joke.

I didn't put the phone number in because if you really cared, I would give it to the person that wanted it.

I gave Shirley my number. She called me and we spoke for several hours. She sounded just like an investigator. I found that amusing. I told her that my name was Reynold.

We went out a couple of nights. We always had great conversations.

Guess what? We have been dating ever since.

Chapter 10

At Band Camp

I had just finished training as an Army musician. I was assigned to my first band. Boy, was I nervous. When I'm nervous, I lose my appetite.

I hadn't eaten much before my first performance, which involved standing on a parade square for about an hour and a half.

I blacked out and one of the other musicians saw me swaying and caught me. My saxophone went flying in the air just before I fell.

It took three men to carry me off the square. The first person I saw was Linda. That was when I came out of my dizzy spell. Around were the musicians.

Linda was just standing next to the soldiers who caught me…

We have been together for over ten years. But guess what? We have been married for eight years!

Chapter 11

Found Romance Instead

A few years ago, I flew to Egypt for an archaeological dig. I used my field kit as my second carry-on. Well, just my luck: after a 10-hour plane ride, I discovered the airline lost my luggage.

After filing my report, I went to my hotel to take a shower and long nap. After checking in, I asked the girl at the counter where to go to buy supplies and clothes.

I began explaining to her my experience with my luggage. When I got back from my shopping trip, I found out that my 'roommates' had used my allotted towels.

Anyway, I went back to the front desk to ask for some towels. Just as the clerk was telling me they didn't have any more towels, the cutest guy I have ever seen tapped my shoulder.

He told me that he had some I could borrow. He also told me that he was visiting from Ireland, and that he always brought his own towels while traveling.

Apparently, he heard my story earlier and felt bad for me and wished there was something he could do. So, we went to his room to get the towels.

As we were walking, he invited me out for a drink to help improve my day.

The best decision in my life was to say yes! Why? Because that's, my dear friends, how I met my husband.

Chapter 12

Three Quarters Turned
into Cupid's Arrow.

Bill and I lived in the same college dorm for nearly two years. We have never met before until that day…

When we met, almost four months into the semester, he was doing his laundry. He realized that he needed seventy-five cents to finish his laundry.

He walked around the nearby lobby. He was checking to see if anyone may have any change. I was sitting at a table with friends.

The funny thing is that I never carry my wallet when I am with friends around the dorm.

At that point I saw my wallet. I looked inside and there were three single quarters. Nothing more. Nothing less. I let him have my quarters and we exchanged names.

Four years later, we were exchanging vows. Not a bad deal I would say.

It only took me seventy-five cents to find the love of my life. Wait, did he ever pay me back?

Chapter 13

The Interview

"It was the early 2000's and I was a matchmaker. Like all twenty-something women, I was very popular.

It was around September when I decided to create my matchmaker company. People were always asking me about dating in my hometown, therefore, I took advantage of that opportunity.

The local paper did a full article on me with a big photo. Later that month, I got an email from some radio DJ inviting me on his show for an interview.

I didn't listen to that station, and I had no idea who he was, but my mom said, "Go for it! It could be fun!"

I met Joe the following week for the on-air interview…

I remember very clearly the day I showed up for the interview. Willie was sitting at his desk looking very professional.

I was dressed to kill. I had a beautiful navy-blue suit, black shoes, and the cutest purse. My hair was pulled back. My makeup was very simple, however, I looked great.

Willie took one look at me and was stunned. The interview went very well. Since it was a live interview, people started calling left and right. It was a very productive interview for both Willie and me.

After the interview, we decided to go for a couple of drinks. We were talking like a couple of old friends.

Weeks turned into months. My mother told me that we looked so cute together.

I must admit that I enjoyed his company. Also, let me remind you that Willie worked at a local radio station, and I own a small dating agency. We were well known throughout the whole city…

We were engaged eight months later and will be married twelve years in October. We have three wonderful children.

"I would have missed out on my whole life if I skipped that interview!"

Chapter 14

The Random Number

I was a freshman in college when the funniest thing happened to me....

I was texting my friend Olga. For no reason at all, instead of sending my text to Olga, my phone sent it to a random New York number.

It was a man on the other side. He texted me back asking who was I?

When we figured out the strange phenomenon, he asked me if I wanted to be his friend.

We hit it off there and almost seven years later we got married.

Chapter 15

The Coffee Shop

I was at a coffee shop when it happened....

The place was packed as usual. I stood online and started looking around. I was just looking when I saw the most gorgeous man a few people ahead of me.

We made eye contact a couple times. I couldn't believe that this nice-looking guy was looking at me. My heart was beating out of my chest!

He ordered, I waited my turn and got my own cup of coffee. I walked over to the table where the cream and sugar were kept.

He came over to fix up his coffee. He picked up the sugar bowl and asked me, "Do you take sugar?" To my surprise, he promptly dropped the bowl right at my feet! It covered both our shoes!

We both cracked up and decided to get a table together....

We just celebrated our 3rd wedding anniversary last month!"

Chapter 16

The Dead Car

"I was about to turn 30, so I decided to do something 'fun' every day for the last month of my twenties.

I ended up doing a lot of stupid meet-up things, including a Cards Against Humanity tournament at a pub.

Everyone there was told to make sure their cars weren't parked in a certain lot.

Of course, mine was in that lot, but when I went out to move it, my car was dead.

I had to call for a tow truck, and the minute I met the tow truck driver, I took one look at him, and something clicked in me.

I ended up spending the next two hours with him in the truck, talking, laughing, and flirting HARD.

When he dropped me off at home, I gave him my number. I had just enough time to text my sister and tell her about how thankful I was that my car broke down, when he sent me a text.

We have been together two years now, and he is the love of my life!"

Chapter 17

The Dogs

My husband and I met walking dogs. It was a sunny summer day before my summer college class, and I was walking my roommate's dog.

I had no makeup on, it was my third day of not washing my hair, and I was just thinking to myself how I really needed to look human like for my class while sitting on the grass waiting for the dog to do his business.

Suddenly, I heard someone say hello… and when I looked up, it was a tall, good-looking guy with a Golden Retriever, my favorite breed!

We talked for a couple of minutes while our dogs smelled each other's butts. We each went home.

Soon, we began to secretly anticipate each other's schedules so that we could take our dogs out at the same time and be able to talk.

After running into each other several times, he finally asked me out on a date. Now, a couple of years down the road, we have been blissfully married for five months!"

Chapter 18

The Concert

I went out last-minute to a concert with a friend. I thought I would immediately end up regretting it.

To my surprise, I met a super-cute guy there. We really hit it off. Unfortunately, I was moving to another city.

I told him that nothing was going to come of it… until he told me he lived in the city I was moving to.

He ended up picking me up from the airport when I arrived, and the rest is history."

Chapter 19

The Fateful Match

My now-fiancé and I literally ran into one another while on the same co-ed hockey team.

This was my first match on this new team after just moving to this new state.

I got lost on the way to the rink. I showed up late and didn't have the chance to meet all my new teammates.

We were both skating fast for the puck, so we hit at incredible speed. He jumped up and helped me up.

The moment we looked at each was love at first sight. We were as if we were a relation for a very long time.

We have been together for the last four years. We were love struck after that crash…

Chapter 20

The Non-pet Friendly Hotel

I had just moved to town and my apartment wasn't ready yet. I had to stay in a hotel. The hotel had a strange rooming system. I was in 4B, and the clerk said the door would be cracked open because the cleaning crew had just finished.

I reached a cracked door and assumed it was mine, so I opened it. There was a man standing there with a dog in a non-pet-friendly hotel.

He just looked at me and said, "Please do not tell me! My house is being fumigated and this was the best hotel I could afford!"

I just laughed and said, "Dude, chill. I just moved here, my dogs in the car, I intend on sneaking her in too. Your dog is cute as hell."

We ended up really hitting it off, as did our dogs. He went home the next day, but we exchanged numbers.

On my second-to-last day at the hotel, somebody called in about my dog. They let me stay, but said my dog had to go.

He offered us both a place to crash, which I said was too weird, but they let my dog stay. I ended up dating the guy I me. Guess what? We are still together.

Chapter 21

Low Blood Sugar

Before Juan was my husband, we worked in the same department. I was also part of a medical first response team made up of trained volunteers for on-the-job medical emergencies that might arise.

My Juan is diabetic, and he had low blood sugar. His normal response to a low Sugar level is falling asleep, but on one day at work, he was very animated and laughing and jumping around.

I and a couple other medical team members were trying to calm him down and get him to eat something to bring his blood sugar up. To stop him from running through the facility, I was holding his hand. Once we got him to calm down and sit, I sat next to him and talked.

I may have been flirting a little bit. He was cute, after all. He kept saying he loved my smile and asked why my face was turning red.

Anyway, after that we started to talk at work. A few weeks later he asked me over for dinner. We were engaged three months later.

We have now been together six years and have been married for four. The really crazy thing was that day I was actually supposed to be on vacation, but plans feel through."

Chapter 22

Chemistry Partner

On February 17, 2023, Ana life changed. It was also the day my life changed. It was the day Ana found out she had Leukemia…

The first day of my junior year of high school I had Chemistry first and second period. All I could think when I walked into the lab was how am I going to stay awake?

I saw the teacher standing by the door and walked over to her.

"Name?" she asked with an annoyed tone.

"Allen." I said.

"Allen, do you have a last name?"

"Jones."

"I'm not kidding. Give me your last name."

It took her a moment to check the list and check off my name. She then told me, "See the girl with the blonde hair? That's your lab partner for the rest of the year. No substitutions or swaps."

"Alrighty." I said and grumbled off to meet my lab partner for the rest of the year, no substitutions, or swaps. I sat down next to my new lab partner.

"Hi, I guess you're my lab partner for the rest of the year, no substitutions or swaps." She said with a smile.

"Hi. My name's Allen."

She smiled and laughed. "Well, my name's Ana Cruz. I moved here from New York a few weeks ago. I came from a public school in New York, and I have no clue if I'm going to be able to keep up."

"Well Ana, if you ever need help you know where to find me." We both smiled and began to listen to the lecture.

When Mrs. Brown finally let us loose with the Brunson burners and extremely dangerous chemicals it was chaos.

The table next to us managed to melt the glass beaker spilling all the contents onto the table leaving a small cat sized hole in the lab table.

The table behind us exploded the contents of their beaker everywhere burning multiple innocent bystanders. We weren't doing too well ourselves.

Ana had beautiful long blonde hair and she forgot to tie it back before we started. About five minutes into our experiment, I looked over and her hair was sizzling and smoking.

The smell of her burning hair was overwhelming.

"Ana." I said.

"What?!" She cried. We were both becoming agitated with the assignment.

"Ana!"

"What! Allen?"

"Your hair!"

"My hair? Oh God." She sprayed her hair down with the water that was sitting on our lab table for events such as this.

"Miss Cruz, I see that you did not follow one of my rules. Do you know what the penalty is for not following my rules?"

"Yes, Mrs. Brown." Emma said. People all around Emma and I began to cry.

"And what would that be?" She asked Emma a cruel smile beginning to form on her face.

"I am banned from the lab for the rest of the semester." I couldn't let Ana fail.

"Mrs. Brown, I distracted Emma and she forgot to pull her hair back." I told Mrs. Brown.

"Alright, Allen, detention for a month, Mondays, Wednesdays, and Fridays. I 'll be seeing you after school today to start your detentions." She told me.

"Yes, Mrs. Brown."

"Oh, Ana, next time, I will kick you out of my class." She reprimanded Ana and returned to the front of the room.

When Mrs. Brown's back was turned Ana whispered to me. "You didn't need to do that. It was all my fault. I'm lucky I didn't lose all my hair.

It's a good thing that this happened. I've been meaning to get my hair cut short for such a long time.

This was the extra push I needed." She told me in a rush of words. I had a hard time following her.

"Well, if it counts, I like your hair long." I told Ana. I hoped I hadn't freaked her out. I'd only known her for an hour and a half, and I was already giving her creepy complements.

"Thanks, I'll take that into consideration." She smiled and returned to her lab report.

The bell rang half an hour later and we packed up. I walked her to her locker. I watched her try to pull her books off the top shelf of her locker. She was up on her tiptoes.

I reached up to help her and everything on the top shelf fell to the floor. I quickly stooped to the ground and started to collect her things.

"Calm down. I'm perfectly able bodied and capable of picking up my own books."

She laughed and took her pink notebook from me. She came a step closer, her hair brushed against my cheek, and she whispered in my ear 'thank you' and hurried off to her next class.

I was stunned and shocked. My heart pounded. My palms began to sweat, and the bell rang. I was late for the third class of my junior year.

I couldn't believe that I could have so much homework the first day of school. It was crazy. I slowly walked back to my locker and put what I needed to bring home into my backpack.

There was no need to hurry, I wasn't going anywhere any time soon. I could sense that somebody was behind me. I turned around to see Emma's beautiful smile and golden hair.

"I just wanted to thank you again for covering for me in chem class today.

Before you go report to detention, I owe you big time." She smiled, kissed me on the cheek, and went to her locker to get ready to go home.

I was beginning to wonder if Ana had this effect on all guys or if it was just me.

The next morning, I couldn't get to chem class quick enough. Ana walked in ten minutes later with her hair pulled back into a low ponytail with a ribbon.

It was almost like she was mocking Mrs. Brown. She sat down next to me, my non-substitutable or swappable lab partner.

I could never imagine substituting or swapping Emma for another partner. I hoped she felt the same way.

"I see you remembered to tie your hair back." I said, half laughing.

"Yes, I did." She smiled.

"Your hair looks nice today." I told her.

"Thank you, Allen." She said to me and began to work on our newest lab assignment.

Three broken beakers and two hours later we had successfully completed the experiment and lab papers.

Mrs. Brown came around to our table and looked impressed. She passed by without saying a word.

Ana and I hi fived when she was over reviewing some other kid's experiment.

This little ritual of chem class went on for months. After I finished my detentions, I'd go over to her house, and we would study.

Her mom would make dinner and ask the both of us how our days went. It was the same old answer every day.

One day Ana was showing me this amazing pianist on YouTube, and we eventually ended up on his Myspace.

We scrolled down through his comments and saw this Chris Townsend kid.

Ana clicked on his name, and it brought us to his page. The first song on his play list off his CD was Stay Positive. We listened to it for a bit. The song was amazing and beautiful.

Ana turned to me and said that this would be our song. She also told me that every time we heard this song, we would think of each other. How could I disagree with her?

The last week of Christmas vacation I finally worked up enough courage to formally ask Ana out.

We had gone to many movies and the Christmas Dance together just as very good friends.

We weren't officially "going out" yet. We were sitting in her room reviewing for mid-terms.

"Ana." I called over to her.

"Yes, Allen?"

"I was wondering if you would like to go ice skating with me tonight."

"Like a date?" She asked, turning around in her desk chair to face me.

"Yes."

"I'd love to." She smiled and came over to me and kissed me on the lips.

There was an outdoor ice rink set up for the weekend at the museum in our town. I decided to take Ana there.

Later that day, I picked Ana up at her house. She came down the stairs in an adorable blue jacket and white knit scarf, hat, and gloves combo. We had a great time.

April first came and went without a problem. The next day I went to chem, and Emma was not in her seat.

I worried the whole entire day. After school I stopped by her house and rang the bell.

Ana answered the door and told me to come in. She took me up to her room and told me to sit down.

I did what she said. She did not look like she wanted to be disobeyed.

"Allen, I went to the doctor today." She told me, sitting down next to me.

"And?" I asked trying to prompt her.

"They found something strange in my blood work. Something not good. They say that I have leukemia.

They need to do more blood work but-" I cut her off.

"You have cancer?" I asked.

Ana began to cry. "Yes, I have cancer." She said matter of fact.

"You have cancer?" I said again.

"Yes, Allen I have cancer. There is nothing I can do about it but accept the fact that I have cancer and start an extremely aggressive chemo regimen and hope it works."

"Are you going to lose your hair?" I asked her.

"Yeah. I guess I'm going to get that short haircut that I've been wanting." She laughed.

"Are you going to live?"

"They say I will since I caught it so soon. There is an 85% survival rate."

"There is still 15%."

"I know. I'm going to kick that 15% in the butt and make it wish it never thought of saying I was going to die."

"Are you afraid?"

"I'm very scared. Are you afraid?"

"I think I'm even more scared than you."

In the background I could hear our song playing, Stay Positive, by Chris Townsend.

At the same exact moment, we looked at each other and said, 'Stay positive'. That was the last time I saw Ana cry.

As the days rolled along Ana's hair began to fall out. It started in small patches that she could easily hide by combing her hair differently.

Eventually the bald patches became too noticeable, and she got her head shaved.

One day after school, Ana asked me to let her drive home. I had picked her up that morning and was going to drive her home so we could study but I was too smart to disagree.

She had this determined look on her face, and I wasn't going to stop that.

We pulled up at the local barber shop and she said, "I'm tired of my hair, I'm getting it shaved off and you are going to stand there and help me get through it."

We walked into the barber shop, and she told the man at the front desk, "I have cancer and my chemo, is making me go bald. I want you to shave my head."

The man at the front desk looked at her in utter disbelief. She was a paying customer, and he couldn't argue.

He walked her over to one of the chairs. He turned the electric razor on and began to shave what was left of Ana's golden locks.

When the man was done, she looked at herself in the mirror, handed the man a twenty, and walked out of the shop.

I caught up with her at the car. "Do you want me to drive you home?" I asked.

"I think that would be a good idea." We spent the car ride to her house in silence.

When we got back to her house she walked inside, and her mother took one look at Ana's nearly bald head and hugged her.

Her mother did not cry, she only held on to Ana for as long as she possibly could before Ana broke away.

Ana's mother kissed her on the head and went back into the kitchen.

The next day when Ana and I walked into school, his jaws dropped.

People finally realized what was going on with Ana Cruz. They did not fully understand but they had a better idea now that Ana didn't have hair anymore.

When we walked into the chem class, Ana walked over to Mrs. Brown and just stared at her. Mrs. Brown's jaw dropped, and she never gave Ana any more problems.

Mrs. Brown just looked at Ana with this pathetic look of sympathy and Ana hated that even more than her constant grief.

May came around and prom fever was in the air. Everybody was buzzing. I decided to ask Ana to the prom.

I walked up to Ana's locker at the end of the day as usual and pulled a single daffodil out of my backpack and asked her to prom.

She smiled and kindly accepted the flower and my invitation....

May seventh came rolling around sooner than both of us could imagine.

I picked her up at her house. I watched her come down the stairs in a beautiful corn flower blue silk gown, we stood in front of the mantle in her living room for a quick photo opt, and then we were off to the prom.

We danced. We talked to our friends. We ate and we had a good time. The last song of the night was our song.

We looked at each other and I held her in my arms. I whispered in her ear, like she did to me so many days ago, but the words were different.

I 'love you', I told her. She looked up at me and said, 'I love you too' and rested her head back on my chest.

That summer her cancer took a turn for the worse. The doctors could not seem to get her into remission.

She lay delicately in her hospital bed covered up to her neck in blankets. She was a thin and tired version of the Ana I met so many months ago.

It was August second. I had just come back from eating in the cafeteria at the hospital.

I sat down on her bed and kissed her head. She looked up at me and smiled. Her smile was beautiful. She whispered to me, 'I love you'. The monitors went dead. My Ana was gone…

Chapter 23

The Perfect Relationship

There was once a boy named Ramon. He lived a normal life with a normal girlfriend and the perfect parents in a perfect house. On a perfect street.

His girlfriend's name was Carmen. Carmen and Ramon have been going out for five months. Everything was going great until….

It was a Monday . That dreadful, awful Monday. Monday was the day she was going to meet Ramon.

They were walking down the hallway and Carmen dropped her paper but didn't even know it, Ramon picks it up and says, " Excuse me miss did you drop this".

As Carmen turns around with hesitation, she says flirtatiously, yes, I did.

As Ramon caught her eye. They started talking and flirting and before you know it Ramon asked her out on a date and without hesitation she said yes.

When she went back to class she sat next to James as always but knew she was thinking about Ramon.

James asked Carmen what she was doing tonight. She had to make up a lie because she knew she was going on a date with Ramon.

Now Carmen did like James, but she was bored. She wanted something new, some adventure, and she wasn't interested in James anymore.

She couldn't break his heart. That is the reason she didn't break up with him.

She didn't want to like someone that did not go the way she wanted. She did not want to end up lonely and heartbroken. So, she stayed with him, risking him in finding out about Ramon.

The next morning Carmen called her best friend, Dorothy and told her everything.

Since they don't live next to each other, they can't be there when stuff happens. Dorothy thinks she is going to get caught but lets her do what she wants to cause it's not her relationship.

At school Carmen goes to her locker and gets ready for class. Ramon surprises her by showing up.

As soon as she closes her locker, they mingle with other classmates. They all walked to class.

As they were walking, Ramon invites Carmen to his house for a party he's having on Friday. Hoping she comes he says, please come.

Pondering whether she wants to go, she pauses for a moment and says, sure I'll go, can't wait.

As the day goes on, she spends most of it with James, but he minds totally on Ramon.

Whenever James asks, what is wrong sweetie? She says nothing honey and smiles. The day goes on and she continues to think of him and when she sees him, she can't do anything but flirt and giggle.

Meanwhile James can hint at the difference in Carmen and no matter how he asks the answer is always going to be nothing.

So, one day he is walking through the mall and meets this wonderful, cute girl named Dorothy.

He has no idea its Carmen best friend. The day of the dance comes around. She is excited waiting for Ramon's phone call. She prepares her self-putting on her good perfume and making sure every piece of hair is in place.

She walks down the stairs and paces the floor waiting for the doorbell to ring. The doorbell rings. She pauses and then she goes to it.

She doesn't want to seem like she was waiting, so she hesitates and then it rings again, and she opens it with the fluttering of butterflies in her stomach.

She opens the door and Ramon says you look nice tonight as she turns to get the keys and her jacket.

Hoping he noticed her outfit as, she turned around. He is such a gentleman; she thinks as he opens the door to his car.

She climbs in and they are off to his house for the party. Meanwhile James is getting ready while Dorothy waits downstairs.

James puts on his best cologne and combs his hair and walks downstairs to surprise Dorothy and they are off to Ramon's party.

Ramon and Carmen arrived at the party. As they walked in, Ramon introduced Carmen to everyone.

He shows her the house. Toward the end of the tour, Carmen asks Ramon if there is anywhere, she can put her jacket.

He told her down the hall and to the right. Carmen walks in and puts her stuff down. Ramon told her that he would be right back. The doorbell rang. Little do they know at the door James and Dorothy.

James and Dorothy wait patiently at the door and then Ramon opens it. James and Dorothy walked in and talked to a couple of friends while Ramon goes back up stair to his room where Carmen was waiting.

He walks in and finds Carmen busy looking at his kid pictures he decides to scare her by putting his arms around he says.

Hey hun, having fun? She turns and says yea a little. They both lean in, and they kiss, and they have this wonderful passionate kiss.

Meanwhile James and Dorothy walked around the house…

The door slowly turns, and Ramon and Carmen are on the bed into their kiss, being so close to being caught.

The door is almost open. Dorothy can't wait to go. She began to scream Carmen!

James yells you cheated on me with Ramon! Carmen says you were going to do the same thing with my best friend Dorothy.

Now, don't come at me with that nonsense boy….

Chapter 24

A Night to Remember

It ended with I do …

That's what I think of every time I think of my first date. It was the perfect night, I thought to myself, remembering my first date with my husband John.

It was many years ago, but I can still remember every detail with perfect clarity. I was so nervous because it was my first date with John, who I had been in love with for what seemed like an eternity, but it was my first date ever.

I spent a long time getting ready, straightening my hair, polished my nails, and going through a million outfits.

At about seven, when he was supposed to pick me up, I was finally ready. Before bounding down the stairs, I took one last look in the mirror.

"Perfect," I thought to myself. When I got downstairs, Jose had arrived and was talking to my parents in the living room.

Looking at my parents, I could tell immediately that they liked him, but then again, what's not to like? He was a strong Christian, a gentleman who was nice to everyone, had a great sense of humor, and great looking.

What more could I ask for? I had been good friends with Jose for years, but it was only a couple of days before that we found out we both wanted to be more than friends.

Seeing him waiting for me left me breathless. I couldn't believe it; he liked me more than a friend!

We left shortly after that. He took me to dinner and then to a movie. What we did on our date I realize doesn't sound all that exciting, but it was to us, two sixteen-year-old who were just enjoying talking and being with each other.

It was the perfect night; as perfect as anything in this life can be, everything felt completely magical, like nothing could go wrong!

After the movie, he drove to the beach where we walked hand in hand, talking, and taking in the beauty of the scenery.

After that, he took me home. I didn't want it to end, but after that night, we spent time with each other almost every day, at school, church, and in our free time.

Then, on my 25th birthday, fifty years ago today, on a walk in the park, he got down on one knee and proposed.

Soon after that, we were married, and it has been a miracle ever since. Even now as I look at him, I feel the same love for him I felt then, and I know it's a love from God. It hasn't all been perfect, nothing ever is, but it's been close. It all started with that first, perfect date.

Chapter 25

Sky

My eyes scanned the large classroom. There she is. Her long, wavy brown hair was shining in the sunlight coming through the window.

Beautiful. I smiled as I made my way through the cramped space between the tables. Getting closer, I noticed the book on the chair beside her, saving my seat.

She turned around in her chair and, seeing me coming, smiled a huge smile, moved the book onto the table, and cast her gorgeous sky-blue eyes toward the chair.

It was from this that I gave her nickname, Sky. I know. Original, right? But it suited her, and she loved it.

As always, she was wearing the necklace I had made for her birthday last year, which brought out her eyes wonderfully.

"Morning, Gabe. How was your date?" She waggled her eyebrows up and down a few times. Ugh. Did she have to remind me?

The night before, I had suffered through endless pain and agony on the worst blind date of my life. Because of what she called her "maternal duty" my mother had set me up with the "delightful and charming" Amber-daughter of my parent's affluent neighbors, Stephen, and Linda Snelling.

Amber was, basically, what every guy, but me apparently, would have wanted in a blind date. She was blond, leggy, voluptuous, bad-private-school girl type, and to top it all off--captain of the cheerleading team. Can you say cliché?

"Don't ask."

"That bad?"

"She thought Leonardo de Caprio painted the Mona Lisa."

Sky's sweet, lilting laugh filled the space between us. "Ouch."

"Yeah." I sighed. Ouch indeed.

"You'll find someone." She said as Professor Newmann began the lecture. I wanted to tell her I already had found someone, she just happened to have a boyfriend and was, apparently, completely oblivious to the fact that I had a Y chromosome.

I had been in love with Sky since I first met her in our psychology class at the beginning of the year.

It was her sophomore and my junior year at Rayford Barnes University, and the seat next to mine was the only one not being occupied.

She stumbled in at the last minute, her hair sticking up, shoes untied, and loaded down with a monstrous backpack and a stack of books in her hand.

Trying to put the books on the table, she swung her backpack around and brained me in the face. When I woke up, the first thing I saw were those dazzling eyes staring down at me. I was hooked.

Since then, I had been upgraded to best friend status, helping with problems, and giving advice, all the while secretly pining like the hopeless loser I am.

As a best friend should, I learned every possible thing about her. Things not even her boyfriend knew. She had been diagnosed with acute lymphoid leukemia when she was ten years old and had a complete remission.

She still slept with her teddy bear, Ernest, that she got for her third birthday. Everything from her favorite color viridian. This is the color you would get if you mixed her sky-blue eyes with my dark green ones, to her first kiss, junior year, YMCA parking lot, Redmond Wiler his real name, believe it or not.

She liked her jeans to fit, loose in the thigh, low on the hips. I could tell you anything. I was overjoyed to be her friend, I really was. I just longed for something more.

I felt something warm on my hand. Glancing down, I saw Sky's hand resting on mine, and I felt a jolt of electricity charge through my veins.

"Gabriel?" Professor Newmann was right next to my desk, a knowing expression on her face. It was beyond obvious that this wasn't the first time she had tried to get my attention, which probably explained Sky's hand on mine.

Glancing over at her, I could see that she was slightly worried, unlike Professor Newmann, who was smirking at me. She was incredibly young for a professor—probably in her mid-thirties and wore different rims around her glasses every day.

This was my second semester of psychology with her, and I had never seen her wear the same ones twice. They were all different colors and shapes.

Some had leopard print or rhinestones. It was as if she used them to see inside our heads. She was one person you couldn't keep secrets from, which, I guess, made sense, her being the psychology teacher and all. Even now, as she looked at me, I could tell she knew how I felt about Sky.

"Sorry, what was that?" I managed, trying to concentrate on talking, rather than the fact that Sky was touching me.

"Your homework, Gabriel." Professor Newmann said gently as she rolled her eyes. It was all I could do not to moan out loud when Sky removed her hand so that I could grab my bag.

I fumbled for the right papers and handed them to her, trying out what I hoped was an apologetic smile.

As she took them, she shook her head in a will-he-ever-learn kind of way. Moving to the front of the room, she sighed and ran a hand through her thick, black hair before turning back to face the class.

"Please turn to page 253 in your books and we'll get started." she said calmly. I read the title of the page we were about to study, Social Influences on Love and Mate Selection. No freaking way.

Chapter 26

My Miracle

There once was a boy named Michael. Michael was the type of boy that enjoyed playing sports at school and being with his friends. He was outgoing and nice until his mother passed away after dropping him off at school.

Ever since Michael lives with his sister, not with his father because his dad supposedly went away for a while or at least that's what they tell Michael, but he knows his dad ran away because he was scared of taking care of two kids by himself.

At school Michael doesn't really have a lot of friends as a matter of fact he doesn't have any, he lost them all after his mother because he just didn't care.

Michael went from being the kid everyone wanted to know to being the loser that no one wanted to talk to.

That was when it all started to change.

Michaels first appointment was on a weds day "the tip of the week" as his mom used to say so they went to the appointment.

Michael didn't really know what to expect he thought it was going to be some lame guy always saying, " so how do you feel about that?"

Michael got to the office and waited to be attended. Minutes passed and he was called by a man with gray hairs all over, he had a long white jacket and asked me to come in with him the doctor took him to his office and said "please sit" Michael sat down on his creamed colored sofa.

The doctor said "hello Michael, I believe you are depressed or at least that's what I read I am Dr. Casten, and I want to help you from what I see you loss your mother.

You need someone to love you as she did, and that love was so great you sister just can't replace it ".

"Ok so," said Michael with an attitude. "Michael I'm trying to help you I'm not going to be your enemy or force you to do anything that's at least what I wasn't to accomplish so how did this begin?" asked Dr. Chasten."

"Well it all started a day after school", Michael went on and told him the sad story by the end the doctor said "Michael as I told you before the only thing you need is someone to love you like your mom did."

Michael said doctor whatever your name is, this is my mom we are talking about you just can replace that, she was my best friend.

My best man or in this case woman. I could go to my mom for anything and everything I loved her, and I will never love anyone like I loved her. It would take a miracle that only the lord and his angels can make possible, maybe not even then.

I loved my mother like I love no one else and now she's gone, and I wonder why sometimes, sometimes I wonder if I did something wrong or if I could have helped her more when she needed my help maybe this would have never happened if she didn't have to take me to school in the morning maybe if …

The doctor quickly stopped Michael and said "Michael one important thing you have to understand is that your moms death was not your fault god has a time for everyone and it was her time I'm so sorry"

"I said it once and I will again. It would take a miracle for me to love someone as much as I loved my mom. " Michael said and walked away.

Ever since Michael told his sister about that appointment, he never went back. He received various calls from the doctor's office, but he ignored all of them.

So, he continued going to school and living his life until one day this girl came up to him, she said " hi I'm Kelsey what's your name?" Michael said " Michael," not only was she cute Michael thought but she came up and talked to me .

Michael got excited and listened to what she said, " I'm new here you think you can show me around?"

Michael was so busy staring at her he didn't answer " Michael so will you show me around?" she asked again " what huh yeah sure" Michael responded, "ok then see you tomorrow."

Michael rushed home, did his homework, and went to bed, he couldn't wait to show Kelsey around school.

When he got to school Thursday morning there, she was waiting for him and she said, "Michael, you made it that's great so where's the science lab that's my 1st class."

Michael spent the whole day with her even at lunch he was surprised she didn't have any friends she was pretty and nice nothing was missing but a posy to follow her around.

Michael and she made a promise that day to sit together at lunch every day so that's how it went.

Months passed and Kelsey knew more and more about Michael than he ever thought she'd know she even knew about his mom.

The funny thing was she was so like his mom he was starting to think a miracle was happening.

He was sure that all this was a miracle when Kelsey said the exact words Michaels mom told him days before her death they were, "when life gives you a hundred reasons to cry think of a thousand reasons to smile."

After Kelsey said those words, Michael told her Kelsey you're my miracle and leaned forward to kiss her. Ever since those words Kelsey and Michael have been dating inseparable ever since.

Chapter 27

Highschool War story

A story cannot be completely true, for the truth is called fact, and fact is boring. To tell my true high school war story I must wrap and fold the truth in embellishment. Transform monotony and routine into fairytale and adventure.

Stories are meant to carry the mind from the usual. In high school there was one thing that made my mind soar and melted away the troubles of life. There is no emotion in the world such as love.

The story I laid before you is one of struggle and heartbreak, of the fine line between love and hate.

I first met him on one of those perfectly hazy mornings where the horizon is lost in fog. Where the place land meets sky is nothing more than a silver sliver.

We spent the boat ride talking, wind in our hair and smiles on our faces. I was young and trapped and he was a free spirit.

He was like no one I had ever met, completely aware of himself with no regard to the thoughts of others, and I, was jealous. All my life I had worried about other opinions, based my interests on what I thought they would accept.

I hid my true self and masked it with what I felt others wanted. He, however, seemed to act against the masses.

There was an instant magnetism between us. We were opposites yet, we fit as if created specifically for the other. His weaknesses were my strengths and what I lacked he possessed in excess.

He took my hand, his eyes burning into mine and promised no matter what, I'll make this work.

He kept his promise. We spent every waking moment in each other's arms and for a time, life was perfect. He was my best friend, my mentor, my hero, and my therapist. He was my first love.

Love, it is a small simple word. A word that holds the indescribable emotion of countless sweethearts that came before, of the endless stream that will follow.

Looking at him, being with him, I felt undying admiration, the utter infatuation, the complete serenity of every love that ever was.

Sometimes I felt I might burst with emotion and the memories of my heart would illuminate the night such as no star ever could.

I honestly believed my soul had found its match and we would float through life to our ever after hand in hand. I know but my heart was content.

On a humid summer afternoon, my world, the one I had grown so accustomed to, dropped out from underneath me. He stood at my door disheveled and dripping with sweat and tears and guilt.

My heart dropped to my feet and with one glance I knew my life would never be the same. I asked what was wrong.

He shook his head and with a mournful sigh muttered, barely audible, "I can't do this." He turned quickly and was gone. I stared after him for a moment frozen in fear, and shock.

I didn't even realize my feet were moving until I noticed houses and trees blur past. I was running, desperately trying to catch what I had already lost.

When I found him, he was under a canopy of trees. Sun streaming onto his face cradling magnitude of the moment. It had been too long, we were too young, were the excuses he gave me.

I never knew love had a time limit. He pulled me in for one last embrace and we stood there, on the gravel path, beneath the trees and the sunlight and I never wanted to let go.

I left him there and walked home alone. The same path that had taken seconds before lay ahead of me never-ending. I finally reached my room and collapsed on my floor and did not move for days. Every ounce of strength was drained.

For weeks I was unable to sleep or eat. I didn't want to see or speak to anyone. The pain was unbearable, and I slowly became numb.

I was crushed under the weight of my thoughts and memories. It was a paralyzing sadness that gripped my heart and made me believe I was nothing.

I hated him for doing what he did. I wanted to go back in time and change things, make things better.

Mend the gaps that had grown between us and live in bliss again. I wanted him to care, to miss me, to want me.

Most of all I hated myself. Hated myself for caring, for not being what he wanted, for losing him. I believed for a long time that I needed him to be happy. That without him I was nothing.

Slowly I came to realize that fighting a losing battle was pointless. That what had happened can never be erased.

I began to live again. He opened my eyes in more ways than one. Because of him I no longer take the little things for granted.

Every moment is a gift to be cherished and not one second should ever be wasted.

Now I view autumn leaves spiraling down with awe and soaking up the rays of the burning sun eagerly.

I listen to the people around me and realize each has a story, a history that I will never understand. He taught me that who I am is all I ever need to be and changing for anyone else is pointless.

I was no longer mourning his loss. He was my first love but there will be more to come. I am who I am because of my past.

Each day builds upon the experiences of the last. Looking back now with tear-filled eyes a smile dances across my lips. For I know the heartbreak was worth the memories.

Chapter 28

A Bit of Fresh Air

Angelina was asleep,..before, but she isn't now. Good Sheppard's Mission in Fort Defiance wasn't exactly a Marriott, and it was showing in everyone's joints.

Angelina was just blessed with scoliosis and an unfortunate memory span. She forgot her 'special' pillow at home probably a estimation of 1000 miles away in Nebraska. She also forgot her blow-up mattress wasn't up to standard quality anymore.

This would be why she's not asleep anymore. Sleeping on the ground on a deflated mattress was in all ways the opposite of restful.

This usually also called for angry tears and anxiety that thus led to running down three flights of stairs and bursting through the front doors into the widely spaced porch.

Not sleeping anymore. Quite the reverse.

Carlos was asleep....before, but he isn't now. Not when his freaking male bladder was bugging him!

Plus, all the dude bathrooms were downstairs cause the little girlies had to have showers upstairs.

All for the sake of women. It was early enough, he could be a little sexist, but no denying girls were nice. Hint.

Clad only in boxers and an undershirt, very attractive, he ventured down the cold steps to the bathrooms in a daze.

Suddenly, through the haze, a noise reached him. It was faint at first but grew as he became more and more awake.

At first it sounded like bells chiming, like someone laughing, but it got deeper and more woeful. Somebody was crying outside- a girl was crying.

"What in the... " He muttered and turned his back on the urinal. Still a little groggy, Carlos saw someone through the windows on the porch.

The picture got cleaner and cleaner with every step until he had pushed the doors open and was on the porch.

The door squeaked open, and Angelina was not alone anymore. Her head shot up and around and frankly found Carlos.

"Carlos?" She whispered.

"Angelina?" He said slightly confused. "What are you doing out here?"

"I...uh... I was, well-" She stuttered. How embarrassing would be to say she was crying, but she didn't have to say anything.

Fully alert now, Carlos noticed the gleaming diamond trails on her cheeks.

"You were the one crying?" He asked

'No hiding it now.' She thought.

"Y-yes." She choked. Quietly, Carlos walked a little closer. Angelina and he were newfound friends, and he didn't want to see her cry.

He placed a warm hand on her shoulder and offered up a smile.

"Want to tell me why?" She shook her head, no. "It'll make you feel better."

"D-doubt it," she muttered.

"Well how else am I going to make you happy? I got to know what magic to throw out." He joked, and she couldn't help but giggle a little.

Carlos might have been a big guy, but his touch was gentle as he pulled her into his big bear hug.

"Is this good?" He asked as she hugged back.

She didn't want to answer verbally in case her voice betrayed her. So, she just nodded furiously. This was extremely good.

He laughed at her childness. She wasn't usually like this. Angelina was more the one to comfort than be comforted.

She's the type of girl who would rather fish and play football than do her hair or paint her toenails. That was totally the girl for him. A moment passed.

"Ready to tell me yet?" She shook her head with the same answer.

Carlos was a great guy. He wasn't overly popular or cocky or typical guy.

He was more of the best friend ever. Like the type who will only date his future wife and is loyal to anyone and everyone. Voted the most dependable...in her book anyway.

Perhaps it wouldn't hurt to tell him...' She didn't think he'd laugh.

"I...I just am.... angry." She whispered

"At whom?" He asked, not laughing. Pause.

"At my blow-up mattress." She heard him chuckle, but she was giggling too.

"Not keeping air in it anymore?" He asked.

"Not at all." She confirmed, and pulled away a little

"But that's only a tiny reason," Carlos said slyly. "You weren't crying over a deflated mattress.

I think I know you better than that." And he held her there. "Problems in your room?" he guessed.

"No."

"Hate the food?"

"Yes and No." She giggled

"Trouble back in the corn?"

"No."

"Boyfriend drama?"

"No!" She cried a bit too quickly.

"It is isn't it?" He smiled, perhaps a little falsely. "What's the situation?"

She grunted and blushed.

"Lack of." She said, but he didn't follow.

"Of what?"

"Of a boyfriend," She sighed. Pause

"Oh..." He breathed.

"But that's not my problem!" She said quickly. That was a little awkward...

"What could it be then?" He rubbed his chin playfully. "I don't see you as the type to get home sick."

He took one look at her expression and knew he'd hit a homerun.

"You're homesick?" he asked a tad bewildered.

"I just miss my parents." She said quietly.

"Well Abby's mom is here. She's like your second mom, you couldn't feel that bad." He spoke.

"I know..." She shrugged. "It's nothing huge, there was really no need for the water works."

She silently looked for any escape. "I guess I'll head back to my flatbed now."

"Are you running away from me?" He asked, but this time she couldn't tell if he was serious or not.

"No" she said.

"Ahm...because I really didn't place you as the track and field type either." She cocked her head at him.

"What's that supposed to mean, Papi?" She used his nickname...the one he hated. She took a step back towards him.

"Well," He took his own step, "I'm pretty good with problem solving."

"And?" She wasn't following.

"I don't know but I think I can solve your shortage." He smiled... but she still wasn't tracking.

"My shortage of what?" She asked.

"Your lack of boyfriend. I'm pretty sure I can fix that."

The two stared at each other.

"F serious?" She suddenly laughed.

"Well as serious as I can be." He smiled and pulled her back to his hold. It was quiet again.

"You think they would consider this purpling'?" She asked.

"Oh yes, definitely." He chuckled.

"Well... I don't think so." She smiled mischievously. He looked at her sly face and smirked.

There's someone I recognize' He thought.

"And what would you say purpling' entitles?" He asked, hopeful of the outcome.

"This." and guess what! They purpled....

Chapter 29

No more

He looked at the black Mercedes. She was gone and all he could do was to look, to watch, to stare.

It started raining again, but he did not notice. She was gone. What else could he do now? No more walking around the flower shop and smelling the sweetness of the spring flowers.

No more going into the kitchen of his father's candy shop to steal the candies he has just baked. No more tree.

It seems like they've spent the entire summer under that tree. They just walked to the park and sat.

They used to sit under that same tree day after day, used to eat the candies he'd just stolen and talk until the sun decided to hide itself beyond the mountains.

They always wanted more time. He wanted to admire those green eyes and she wanted to look at his silly smile. Just a little more, he thought. Just a little.

But the moon was already crossing the sky and the stars already started to appear in the dark-blue sky. It was time to go. Then he guided her across the streets, where earlier children played soccer.

He took her home, gave her a goodnight kiss and walked home. As he crossed the empty streets, he was already thinking about spending the day with her tomorrow.

But no more because now the black Mercedes was crossing the same streets where he'd guided her. He could see on the window of the black Mercedes the girl looking at him.

He could see as the green eyes, he'd admired so much, watered. He wanted to kiss her once again and hug her and say goodbye.

But no more. The black Mercedes turned the corner in the end of the street and disappeared into the rain and the night.

All he wanted was a little more time with her. But the sun was already hidden between the mountains and now the stars did not appear.

They wouldn't, because now a storm was approaching. He wanted to see the sun, the moon, the tree, and those green eyes again.

But no more. It was cold, raining and she was gone. His father guided him across the pavement into his house.

'Come on', he said as he guided his son back home. 'You have school tomorrow.'.

Chapter 30

The Blue Rose

It was there, right they were within her grasp. She reached for it, feeling like her gloved hands were going in slow-motion.

She picked up one of the coveted Count Alejandro's blue roses from the delicate porcelain vase they were always in.

"What have we here?" said a dark, deep voice from behind her. She froze, not even needing to turn around to know who said it. Count Alejandro had a voice that no one could make a mistake.

She clutched the rose to her chest and bolted for the window.

"Oh, that won't do, we can't have you leaving. All the windows are locked and besides we are two stories off the ground."

She could hear the mocking tone in Count Alejandro's voice. But she still tried to pry open the window, despite the Count's words. But it was locked, she contemplated jumping through the glass, but he was right about the height of the window as well.

"Alright now that we've gotten that out of the way tell me, who are you? What are you doing here and why are you taking one of my blue roses? Those are only given to maiden's I find...suitable." He chuckled for some reason.

"But I suggest you return that and tell me who you are, young man." He continued.

Figuring she should salvage what dignity she had left the intruder turned around to face the Count. She threw back her black hood to reveal her face.

The girl investigated the Count's face, realizing he wasn't much older than her, and abnormally handsome. He had a long face with sharp angles.

He looked stern but not harsh. Count Alejandro noticed then the young man' was a beautiful young woman with dark auburn hair and hazel eyes.

She looked like she might have a fever, with her rosy cheeks and sallow complexion. He was intrigued.

"My apologies, milady but your clothing isn't very…well lady like." His eyes looked over her black pants and baggy black jacket.

"You know there are easier ways to get one of my blue roses and attention." He chuckled again but was growing agitated.

"Alright, enough with the silence what is your name?" He was serious now.

"Carina" she said.

"Carina? Hmm, that is an odd name." He said.

"That is my name." Her voice had an edge to it, she didn't like how he implied that it wasn't.

"Alright, alright, far be it from me to say it isn't." He still sounded as if he didn't believe her.

"Tell me, Carina, why are you in my house?"

"Why do you think?" She held the rose slightly out to him before her eyes softened as she looked at it.

She brought it to her nose and breathed in.

"Their smell is one of a kind." Carina looked up as he said this to see his eyes had softened as well.

"Listen, if you send me to jail can you vouch for the death penalty?" Carina asked him her voice still soft and serious.

Taken aback he asked her, "Don't you mean you don't want the death penalty?"

"No, I'll be dead in a week, and I'd rather die by the swift justice of the law than by what would inevitably happen anyway." She sounded so calm it unnerved Count Deion.

"Oh, and is that why you came here? To die?" His voice had a new edge.

"No, I came to live." She sounded tranquil. Recognition dawned on his face.

"Oh, I get it, you came here to find the mysterious Count Deion, and find out whether the rumors are true if I am a vampire.

Then you planned on having me turn you into a vampire as well. I am right?" Carina knew of the rumors that flooded the town.

"As if I would give in to such foolish rumors. I came here for the rose." She said, stroking the soft petals.

"Oh, and now that that's all cleared up." He said sarcastically.

"I was sent by someone, he said he'd marry me if I brought him a blue rose."

"So, you just want to marry the rich man. Or is he going to kill you if you don't marry him?" It seemed odd that this idea would make him angry.

"No, he's not going to kill me, not the fever will overcome me within the next few days that will kill me. It'll be a slow death, and I need…"

Carina could feel her fever rising, her knees buckled under her, and she fell to the carpet. Count Deion rushed over to her.

"Carina, what's wrong."

"Few days, few minutes. Again, death penalty, please." And then everything went black.

Awoke later, but not where she expected she would be. She wasn't on a hard bed in a gray room. Her fever was still raging but she knew she wasn't delirious.

She wasn't giving up the theory of delusion because, instead of being in jail, she was in a cozy bed, covered in thick fluffy sheets.

The room was white, and the curtains were lacy and were pulled over the wide windows with a window seat below it. Looking at all the lace throughout the room Carina groaned.

"What is it? Are you in pain?" asked a concerned voice from near the door of the room. It was Count Deion; Carina couldn't understand why he looked so anxious, why it looked like he cared if she was in pain.

"No, no, I'm fine." Carina started to push the covers off her to get up.

"What are you doing?" he asked appalled.

"Leaving" she replied.

"In your condition?"

"You haven't sent me to jail yet, and I don't intend to stay and wait for you to change your mind." As she sat up, Carina felt like a huge weight was pushing her down. The fever was raging but she tried to fight it.

"Please lie down and listen," The Count placed his hand lightly on her shoulder and gently, but firmly, pushed her back down. Carina frowned as she gave in and laid her head on the soft pillow.

"Now, I'm not going to notify the authorities about your…visit. I have had the doctor come to look at you.

He gave me some medicine and his word that you would be over your cold within a week. Until then you will be staying here." He gave her a sly smile.

"No, that won't do. I should go." Summoning her strength, Carina pushed off the covers and slid off the bed.

But she started to sway and cough uncontrollably, her whole head was burning with the fever. Count Deion caught her before she hit the ground.

He helped her back to bed, though her ragged breathing didn't subside.

"Alright, now stay in bed. You are in no condition to go anywhere now and if I must, I'm willing to call the doctor so you can be sedated." A devilish smile played on his lips, and he chuckled.

"But…I…need to…." She stammered, trying to find a good excuse but her brain came up empty.

"Sleep or be sedated. Either way you will rest." The smile was getting on Carina's nerves. She sighed and said, "Fine" She was past trying to fight against her eyelids.

Her breathing slowed and Count Deion watched her as she slipped into sleep. Lying there she looked even more beautiful. What am I doing? He thought.

Count Deion knew what he should do but the thought tore him up inside. NO! He pushed the other ideas away as they threatened to take root. As soon as she's better I'll let her go.

He promised himself. He let out a sigh and started to leave but couldn't help casting a last glance at Carina's sleeping form.

Before he knew what he was doing, his lips were brushed against hers in a kiss. He softly, but swiftly, pulled her away and left her to sleep.

When Carina awoke again it was about midday. Though what day it was she had no idea. She was feeling better, but the fever was still pounding through her head. Though it wasn't so bad as to leave her in an unsteady state.

She glanced around the room to realize that she really was in a white and pink room that was filled with lace and fluff, this time she couldn't blame it on the fever. Carina frowned.

"What's wrong now?" Carina looked over at Count Deion who was standing in the doorway.

He was trying to look annoyed, but the amusement was slipping though, but an underlying emotion was there that Carina couldn't identify.

"It's too pink and lacy. Oh, and I really hope you are not the one who changed my clothes."

"No, my one of my maids did that. Do you really think so little of me?" He really looked insulted now.

"It's always good to check. Especially when you're in a strange, single man's house and incapacitated."

"You're sick, I hardly think any man would take advantage of you then." He shook his head. "Oh, and what, may I ask is wrong with the room's décor?"

"Pink, I hate it. Pink, decorations, anything too girly." She shuddered. Count Alejandro raised an eyebrow.

"Well, that would explain your original clothing." He chuckled. "Now, I would like to get your story straight. You came to my home to steal one of my precious blue roses because a man said he'd marry you if you gave it to him.

That part is clear, but now tell me do you know the man well?"

"Nope"

"But you must really like him to be willing to break into a house to win his hand."

"Nope"

"Excuse me?"

"I don't know him well and but don't dislike him. I wouldn't say I hate him though. But he's Bartello Mevidue."

"A Mevidue? One of richest families in this part of the country. Impressive." He was seething, Carina could hear it in his voice.

"And what's wrong with wealth? You, yourself are extremely wealthy."

"But I didn't marry someone I didn't even know to get it."

"Alright, you want to know why I'm marrying him? It's because I'm a dirt-poor orphaned girl with no job or home. I'm not that pretty and not that smart. To top it all off I'm a very sickly person.

My immune system is so bad I get colds like this on a regular basis. I've pretty much run out of any scarce amounts of money I had so now I'll either die of sickness or starvation.

"So instead of that I've decided to at least to make one person happy, he even seems to like me, and I won't die. It's a win-win situation." Carina gave a hard laugh which turned into a cough.

"But will you be happy?" He looked at her with his dark eyes, his black hair lining his gorgeous face. Carina mentally shook her head to clear it.

"Happiness, I'm past trying to find that. A handsome, kind man is willing to overlook the fact that I'm plain, poor and without a family or dowry, and still want to marry me is a miracle.

I'm pretty good with that." Carina didn't look at him when she said this. She felt shallow and weak, not to mention telling her sob story to a stranger was not helping her feel better.

Count Alejandro was getting annoyed, with all her answers, and saying how she gave up on trying to be happy. But especially how she kept saying how she was plain!

Count Alejandro was having trouble controlling his temper…

"The maid will be up in a minute with your medicine. Good day." Count Alejandro's eyes had taken on a darker shade and his voice an edge.

Carina couldn't figure out why he was so upset. But he left the room with a noble flourish of his coat.

Carina couldn't explain the shiver of fear that ran down her spine when she thought of the look in the Count's eyes. She brushed the feeling off as side effects of fever.

Just as Count Alejandro said, the maid came and gave Carina a brown liquid that tasted worse than it smelled, and it smelled horrid to begin with. The maid was a plump woman with a kind smile.

The maid put her hand on Carina's forehead and said, "Good, good your fever is down. I really will never understand my lord. He is such an odd one, taking you in like this. You are a sweet girl, but it really isn't like him. I worry sometimes."

"Why is something wrong?" Carina asked her.

"Oh no, but my lord never shown any interest in finding a wife, like any other young man.

Not only that but he's a man of a highly marriageable age. Yet he never attends parties or even shows an interest in a woman.

Well, at least he wasn't until a few days ago." She gave Carina an accusing look.

"Are you suggesting he's shows an interest in me? I'm sorry but that isn't anywhere near his feelings for me.

Pity is there, and maybe annoyance at my inability to recover as fast as he would like but not interest." She shook her head.

"Well, my lord certainly isn't one to wear his heart on his sleeve, but I've been in this house long enough to tell if he fancies a girl.

The fact that he let you stay and recover instead of sending you away is proof enough."

"But-" Carina started to say but was cut off by the maid,

"Now, now settle down. We don't want to aggravate your cold. I'm sure sooner or later we will find out who is right."

She smiled and walked to the door, only to stop and turn back to Carina with a concerned look.

"Oh, and for your own safety don't go out of the room after midnight, especially on the night of a new moon.

Dear me, that starts tonight. Stay in your room alright?" The maid looked worried.

"Alright." Carina agreed, not knowing the significance.

"Promise, me. Promise you will not leave this room after midnight." Her seriousness took Carina off guard.

"Okay I promise." She said, nonetheless. The maid nodded and left the room. Carina was puzzled but determined not to leave the room after midnight.

But Carina's fever was still draining her strength, making her must rest longer. Luckily, sleep came quickly and deeply.

"DAMN IT!" Count Alejandro shouted. He punched the wall in frustration. He looked at the hole he left in the wall. His hand didn't even sting. "God dammit" he mumbled to himself.

How could I do this to her? Count Alejandro thought. He glanced at the clock cursing himself as the hands reached towards 11:30.

"DAMN IT ALL!" he shouted again as he stalked out of the room down the stairs to a room in the basement of the mansion. It was where he would spend the rest of the night, at least he hoped.

"Well, honey I guess I was right." said the maid the next day to Carina.

"About what?" asked Carina as she swallowed a bite of soup.

"My lord Count Alejandro's feelings for you." She replied sounding smug.

"What do you mean?" Carina sounded skeptical.

"Honey, tell me, did you hear any strange noises last night?"

"Strange noises? Like what?"

"Oh… well…" It looked like the maid was thinking then her eyes brightened and said, "Some say the mansion is haunted and every new moon, strange noises can be heard from deep within the mansion."

"Have you ever heard anything?"

"Of course, honey. I've lived here since I was only a couple years older than you. I've heard the noises almost every new moon.

Well, except for last night." The maid gave Carina a knowing look.

"What does that have to do with Count Alejandro's feelings for me?"

"Honey, it's obvious, my lord-" but the maid was cut off by a voice from near the door.

"I think that's enough Ellen." Carina turned to see Count Alejandro standing in the doorway, a poisonous look on his face.

"Yes, my lord." She took Carina's empty bowl and walked out of the room, looking annoyed. Count Deion turned his gaze on Carina.

"She has an overactive imagination. I would suggest you not listen to her." He was still fuming.

"Well, it shouldn't matter soon anyway. I'm almost well, so I should be able to leave soon." She said, unable to meet his dark eyes.

"And who said I would allow you to leave?"

"But why wouldn't you let me leave?" Carina asked, amazed. She looked at Count Alejandro to see if he was joking.

He kept his face blank, but his eyes still shone with anger.

"You do owe me for the medicine and the doctor. To repay your dept I think you should stay here for a while until you've paid it off."

"I guess that is fair. But what do I have to do?"

"Hmm, how about a bet? If your…fiancée, the Mevidue, if he comes to get you then you may go with him. But if he leaves you here then here is where you shall stay, until I let you leave."

"Okay you have a deal" she said.

"Good." But he sounded undecided.

"But tell me, why are you so angry? Was it something I said yesterday?" Carina searched her memory trying to see if something she said could have upset him. Count Alejandro sighed, put his hand over his eyes, and said,

"No, no, but I do wish you'd be more concerned of your happiness. But that really isn't any of my business, is it?" He gave her a hard smile, that made Carina's heart ache with its bitter loneliness.

"If you're worried about me then it's very kind of you but not necessary. I'm nothing special, nothing worth worrying over. I mean I'm happy enough to be alive.

For now, that's all I'm asking for. I'm not about to start hoping just to have those hopes come crashing down and bury me."

Count Alejandro felt a new flare of anger wash through him.

"You really believe you aren't worth having a happy life?!" His voice was loud and harsh.

"You have a chance at living! You could be more than just happy! But you insist that you don't deserve it!

If you don't deserve it, then who does? I'm the last person who deserves it, yet it's still thrust upon me.

If I get a little glimmer of it than you should get a lifetime!"

"And why wouldn't you deserve it?"

"I deserve nothing! I am horrible, a MONSTER!" his voice seemed to shake the room, and Carina along with it.

A furry cough ripped through her. The furious look was replaced by a worried one on Count Alejandro's face.

He reached towards her but dropped his hands in anguish and turned to walk out the door, slamming it on his way out.

Count Alejandro found the maid, Ellen, and told her to assist Carina.

"Oh Dear!" Ellen said as she walked into Carina's room.

She put her hand on Carina's forehead, only to pull it away abruptly. "You poor thing! Your fever is back and just as worse as it was before.

Lay down and I'll be back in a minute with your medicine." She bustled out of the room.

Carina's breath came in long rasps, feeling like her head was about to split in half.

Carina indefinitely remembered the maid coming back and giving her the medicine.

The rest of the day was filled with irregular sleep. In her dreams a shadow was stalking her and a man with dark eyes.

It was that night that Carina heard the screaming. The gonging of the clock rang through the house as cries from what could never be mistaken for human, clashed with the bells.

A cold sweat ran down her neck as the cries became roars. Carina threw the covers over her head.

She knew it wouldn't hold back whatever was out there from harming her, but it helped her nerves.

Then it was silent, only the autumn wind could be heard. Yet, Carina felt even more uneasy, like a darkness had descended upon the house.

Carina was too afraid to fall asleep, but her fever was draining what little energy she had, forcing her to sleep. Only to have nightmares relentlessly haunt her.

The next morning Ellen was fussing over Carina, saying,

"Honey, you look horrible!" Carina didn't even want to think about what she looked like, how her tiredness was bound to leave her with huge purple shadows under her eyes. Not to mention the fever was bound to leave her with a horrible complexion.

"I didn't sleep well." Carina sighed.

"Why honey?"

"I heard the screaming you were talking about."

"Yes, my lord dismisses any servant who wishes to leave at night. But I always stay."

"Did you get used to it?"

"Oh, dear no, I don't think it is something you get used to, but I do my best to ignore it."

"But is it really the ghost making the noise?"

"Of course, dear." But she said it with uncertainty.

"Didn't you say that the ghost's silence proved Count's feelings for me? And last night it was anything but silent, so it looks like I was right, he doesn't have feelings for me. Though I don't see how the two are related." But the latter thought was leaving Carina depressed, yet she couldn't figure out why. Her fever was not helping her clarity of thought though.

"I believe it's my lord who is the one quieting the ghost, something must have upset him yesterday and he couldn't attend to the ghost." She gave Carina a warm smile.

"No, I don't think it's because of me." Her little strength was weakening, so her words came out like huff.

"No use in arguing, dear, you're just exasperating your cold." Carina didn't say anything to that, the tiredness and fever combined had put her in a bad mood.

"Alright dear, I'll be off now but if you need anything give a holler." She smiled and left, leaving Carina to her thoughts. The last thing Carina wanted was time to think.

Count Alejandro had been standing near the door for a while, listening to Carina's unsteady breathing. He couldn't face her but wanted so badly to see her face. As Ellen walked by him, she said in a loud voice.

"Good morning my lord." She smiled mischievously as he glared at her. Carina's head perked up at the sound of his name. Count Alejandro gave a sigh and walked into her room.

He bit back a gasp, she looked terrible. Her face was an ashen white, yet her cheeks softened in a blush. The bags under her eyes were worse than he feared. Yet through it all she still looked beautiful.

Carina looked at him then the blush on her face deepened just as she turned her face away from his gaze. Puzzled, Count Alejandro asked.

"What is it?" Carina gave a hard laugh and replied,

"I must look awful." For some reason Carina didn't want him to see her like that.

"You silly girl, you're allowed to look less than perfect when you're sick." He laughed lightly.

"I'm so tired of this, of being sick."

"You'll be better in a few days then you can go back to your usual happy self."

"If I get better."

"What are you talking about? Of course, you'll recover." He replied sternly, but slightly taken aback.

"I don't have the strength left for that."

"Don't talk like that! Fight back! You must've beaten so many more colds that were much worse than this."

"Yeah, but I was never alone with the really bad ones." Her sadness leaked through her words.

"Alone? I'm right here, and if you want me to stay, well than I won't go anywhere." Carina was surprised by the uncharacteristic warmth in his voice. She looked at him to see his eyes were as soft as his voice.

"I'd like that." She smiled. He returned her smile and walked over to the bed, seating himself on the edge. Hesitantly, he put his hand on her cheek, pushing stray hair back. Her eyes widened and Count Alejandro started to pull his hand back.

Carina grabbed his hand before it left her face and held it there.

"Your hand is so cool, it feels good." She said closing her eyes but keeping his hand in hers. He laughed softly and asked, "Wouldn't you prefer a cold towel?" though he dearly didn't want to remove his hand.

"No" it came out as a sigh.

"Alright then, now sleep."

"Promise you won't leave?"

"I promise, not until it is time for me to retire for the evening." She seemed to except that and let her mind drift. Count Alejandro heard her breathing slowly and knew she was asleep. Yet her hands still held his.

He didn't know how long he had stayed there but the sun had set when the maid walked in.

"She finally fell asleep, did she?" Ellen said.

"Yes, I might've left before now if I hadn't promised, or if she had let go of my hand." He looked at her sleeping form, who hadn't once loosened her soft grip on his hand.

"Dear me, she must have very strong feelings for you."

"Feelings? I sincerely doubt that. She just needs me for a place to rest."

"Why is it that neither of you are willing to admit the other has feelings for you?"

"You told her I had feelings for her?" He was angry, that was clear to Ellen .

"You're both so dense, someone has to give you a push in the right direction." She was not so easily intimidated by his sudden flares of anger.

"I would appreciate it if you'd stop telling her things like that." He was still angry, but his voice stayed low, so he wouldn't wake Carina up.

"Why my lord? I am right, you do have feelings for her." It wasn't a question.

"Yes, I think...I think that I love her." His voice was just a whisper.

"I told her, but she wouldn't listen." She sounded smug.

"Good, that's for the best. I forbid you to tell her anything more."

"Oh, I see, you want to tell her yourself." Ellen was brightened at the idea.

"No, she will never hear about my feelings for her, ever. It will be better this way."

"Better? How is letting her stay ignorant to your feelings better?"

"Ellen, she is about to marry a wealthy, normal man who will take care of her.

With him she'll get the best care she can and…and I'll never be able to hurt her. That's all I want, for her to be safe." But it was a lie, he wanted so much more, he wanted her.

"My lord, I believe she would accept you and your dark side."

"NO!" he yelled, then held his breath as he watched Carina, to see if he had woken her.

She stirred but didn't awaken or release his hand. He let out his held breath and said more quietly.

"I will not put her through that. Besides, I know my feelings are one-sided. I am nothing more than a friend to her.

She expects nothing from me but heaven. Therefore, I refuse to even consider bringing her into this."

"And what my lord, will you do if she does return your affections?"

"It's a proposed point. Now," he glanced at the clock and grimaced, "I will need to be preparing for the long night I have ahead."

He looked at Carina, hoping her face would give him strength.

"My lord-" she started in a patronizing voice but was cut off by Count Alejandro.

"Even if she did start to develop feelings for me, what kind of life would she live?

In love with a monster like me, she would never be able to live a normal life. You know I have a terrible temper, what if I hurt her? Besides you saw her this morning, if she stayed here then every time, she got sick it would be my fault she is so tired she considers letting herself die."

He was getting angry again, Count Alejandro took a deep breath trying to calm himself.

"Okay, there is no use in arguing we'll just wake up Miss Carina. I'll see you in the morning, my lord."

Ellen smiled and left the room. The Count gave a sigh and returned his gaze to Carina. Her complexion was back to almost normal and the bags under her eyes looked less purple.

He sighed again and gently extracted his hand from her grasp. His hand felt cold and empty, he clenched it into a fist. His heart did a leap, though when Carina gave a small cry of sadness when he took his hand away.

She looked so distraught that Count Alejandro leaned in and kissed her cheek as he pulled his lips away, he whispered.

"Don't worry, I'll be back in the morning." Count Alejandro almost thought she had woken up because a small smile spread across her face, and she looked content again.

It took all he had not to put his hand back on her cheek and stay there the whole night, he sat up and swiftly left the room. He walked down the stairs to the last room he would see until morning.

"Did you sleep well, honey?" asked Ellen.

"Much better than yesterday, thank you." replied Carina

"You look better to. I'd say you're finally getting over this cold."

"I think so as well about time too. Hey Ellen?"

"Yes honey?"

"Could you do me a favor? Open that window over there? I really want to go outside, I've been sitting here in this bed for too long, but I know that is out of the question." Carina gave a huff.

"Oh, course Dear." She smiled and walked over to the long window and grasped the handles, rattled them a bit and turned back to Carina with a defeated look.

"Sorry honey, but it looks like my lord has them locked."

"Probably to keep me from sneaking out."

"If you had your strength back earlier, I wouldn't have been surprised if you attempted it."

Ellen chuckled and Carina joined her, knowing full well she would have tried it. "I'll go ask my lord for the key." She walked out of the room leaving Carina to contemplate her chances of sneaking out for a minute.

Ellen had said that most of the servants weren't here. She smiled and slipped out of bed. Carina stepped out of the room and slowly closed the door behind her, hoping the lack of noise would not alert anyone to her escape.

"Where are you going?" said a voice from behind her. Carina froze, the voice sounded angry, amused and a hint of hurt.

She turned around to see Count Alejandro glaring at her. He was trying to look amused, but the hurt was plainer in his eyes.

"I figured I'd sneak around until I could find the front door." The pain intensified in his eyes though he raised an eyebrow.

Still trying to look amused, so she continued quickly, "I was not trying to escape mind you, I just wanted to get some air and the ulterior motive of getting a look at the reclusive Count Alejandro's house unsupervised was a highly intriguing idea."

She gave him a mischievous smile. He gave her a disbelieving look. "You don't believe me, do you?" she asked disgusted.

"You are notorious for sneaking around people's houses and trying to leave."

"Hey, I sneak into houses not out of them." He raised the eyebrow further, the pain still in his eyes.

"I promise," she said more seriously, "I was not trying to run away, we had a deal, and I don't plan on backing out. I really hate being cooped up in that room, I just wanted to go outside.

But if you really don't like it, I'll just go back to my room." She turned around to go back into her room, but a hand grabbed her wrist.

Carina looked at Count Alejandro, a questioning look on her face. The painful look in his eyes was gone, that or he had managed to hide it.

"Would like to go outside?" he asked, sounding defeated.

"Yes, very much so."

"Alright then." He gave her his own mischievous smile and before she even realized what he was doing he had one arm around her shoulders while the other swept her feet from under her.

" What are you doing?!" she asked him, appalled. Count Alejandro held her in his arms off the ground.

"Taking you outside. You are still recovering; I refuse you to let you do anything that could aggravate it."

"I can walk on my own." She objected, flustered. Yet a part of her pointed out that she was enjoying it.

"I'm sure you can, for an extent. But the last thing I want is for you to strain yourself and end up sick again." He never wanted to see her like that, not if he could help it.

"Oh, alright." She gave in. He smiled, while his entire being glowed. Count Alejandro started walking down the hall, and into a wide area with the master staircase.

Carina bit back a gasp, it was magnificent. The room looked like it was meant for a grand ball, and probably was.

Tapestries hung on the walls and long windows let light into the room. All the cloth was gold and a redder shade of maroon. Count Alejandro looked at her expression and said,

"Do you like it?" He almost sounded smug.

"It's beautiful." She replied still in awe. He laughed and started to descend the stairs. Carina wrapped her arms around Count Alejandro's neck, clinging to him, feeling uncomfortable with the idea of falling down the stairs to a hard marble floor.

Count Alejandro took in Carina's scent hungrily, she smelled sweet, like honey. Her closeness was lovely, he resisted putting his cheek on her head. When they reached the bottom of the steps he turned right, away from the large front door.

"Where are we going?" Carina asked puzzled.

"It's a surprise." Count Alejandro replied. He carried her down a wide hallway, and at the very end stood a thick oak door.

Count Alejandro set Carina down on her feet and opened the door. Carina gasped, behind the door was a courtyard, covered in flowers of every color.

The smile on her lips sent a wave of joy through Count Alejandro's body. Carina walked into the courtyard, taking in the scents of the multitude of flowers.

Then something caught her eye, in the corner, right up against the wall, were three rose bushes. She walked over to them and sat down, she reached towards one of the roses and stroked the petals.

"Can I have one?" Carina asked Count Alejandro. He smiled at her and nodded. Carina took hold of one of the rose stems,

"Ow!" she said. He was there next to her in an instant.

"What did you do now?"

"It's nothing, I just pricked my finger on one of the thorns. It's just a flesh wound." She held it up him to see. He took her hand in his and inspected the small cut.

Keeping her hand in one of his, he used his other to reach into his pocket. He took out a small black handkerchief and tore it in half with his teeth and tied it around her finger.

"There, now let me get the rose." He reached into the bush and expertly plucked a rose. He proceeded to snap off all the thorns. Count Alejandro then handed her the flower.

"Really, I don't think that was necessary." She said.

"Maybe not, but I don't want to risk you passing out from blood loss."

"I'm not that fragile." Carina protested. Count Alejandro raised an eyebrow.

"I may get sick a lot but I'm not going to faint from a thorn prick." Count Alejandro gave a short laugh and Carina scowled at him. Her eyes drifted towards the rose in her hand. She smiled and inhaled the sense of it. The smell had a nostalgic effect on her.

"You really love roses." It wasn't a question.

"Yes, my…my mother used to have a rose garden. She would always tell me the story of a girl who made the roses bloom, and a demon who loved her."

"Hmm, I believe I've heard this story, but I would like to hear your version." He sounded slightly interested but his eyes held something else.

"Okay, my mom would always start:

Once there was a girl named Rosa,'" Carina noticed Count Alejandro flinched at the name, "There was a barren land where nothing would grow.

Rosa tirelessly worked on the land until finally roses bloomed. A demon fell in love with Rosa and her dedication. The demon proposed to Rosa, she told him that she would marry him but only if he could find her a blue rose.

"The demon searched for the blue rose for many years. Rosa eventually grew old and died.

The demon was so distraught he cried for the first time, his tears soaked the earth and blue roses bloomed, and the demon died." She finished.

"I've always loved the story, but when I was little, I would come up with different endings." Count Alejandro looked slightly annoyed. "What?" she asked him.

"Well, the version I was told was similar, but it was a little different." He said casually.

"Oh? And what were you told."

Well for one thing, doesn't it seem odd that Rosa would send the demon for a blue rose? Before the demon cried there was no such thing, yet Rosa sent him away to find one.

Your story doesn't say what Rosa did all those years while the demon searched. Well, Rosa didn't wait patiently for him to return, no, she married and had children.

She all but forgot about the demon who had sworn his love to her.

The demon, on his search he found a sorceress. The demon truly loved Rosa and wished to be human so she would love him as well.

The sorceress allowed him to appear human but only until midnight then he would revert to his demon form until the sun rose again.

When the demon returned to find Rosa had betrayed him and died, he did cry. But he lived on, searching for the woman that would love him.

Carina took in Count Alejandro's words, looking at the story she grew up on anew.

"You don't have to believe me but…" he trailed off looking torn. He looked at her face, Carina was quiet. It unnerved him.

"Come on let's get you back to bed. We'll leave the window open this time." Carina nodded. Count Alejandro stood up and scooped her off the ground, Carina clutched the rose to her chest. He carried her to her room. Count Alejandro pulled out a key and unlocked her windows.

"Thank you." Carina said.

"Okay, but you'd better not try escaping." He laughed.

"I really don't think you need to worry about that." She gave him a small smile.

Count Alejandro left the room. Carina's quietness had left him disconcerted. He couldn't understand why when he told her the story, she didn't say anything.

Was she angry at him for ruining the story she had known since childhood. Or worse, did she put two and two together? Did she know about him?

He almost ran back into the room and confronted her. He reasoned with himself that wouldn't help, he tore himself away and went to the kitchen, an idea brewing in his head.

A few hours later Ellen walked into Carina's room.

"Well come on let's get you presentable." Ellen said.

"Why? "Carina asked.

"Dear, you're having dinner tonight with my lord."

"I am?" Carina said taken a back.

"Of course, dear, by the master's request. But only if you think you're up to it."

"No, I'll go." For the next half hour Ellen had Carina bathe, she did her hair and had her put on a dress that didn't lack frills.

Ellen then led her down the grand staircase to another large hall with a long table in the center of it.

Count Alejandro was sitting at the opposite end of the table, and right next to his seat was another place setting, her place.

Carina stared at the ground as she walked towards the Count. She couldn't look at him, not in the dress she was wearing.

"What is it?" he asked concerned.

"Did you have to make me wear this?" She asked, fluffing her dress.

"I'd have to say you look lovely." His voice was soft.

Carina blushed. "Come sit next to me." He pulled out her chair and pushed Carina in when she sat down.

In a grand procession the servants came out carrying trays of food, most Carina didn't even recognize. The food all looked so decadent she just gaped at it; her mind couldn't even comprehend what it all must taste like.

Count Alejandro swept a hand above the spread and said, "Dig in." Carina just continued to stare, not knowing where to begin.

The Count pursed his lips. After a few seconds he said, "Alright then I'll start." He grinned and reached over to a plate with some sort of crackers with some white meat on top, maybe fish or even chicken.

She couldn't tell, he popped it into his mouth, chewed and swallowed. "Well, it's not poisonous. I'd say it's quite delicious. Here," he handed her one.

Carina took it, looked at it then put it in her mouth. It was amazing, absolutely melting on her tough.

"It so…good!" she said.

"I'm glad you like it. Have as much as you want."

Carina took a bit of everything onto her plate. Count Alejandro smiled and put various delicacies on his plate.

After a they had been eating for a little while Count Alejandro cleared his throat and said, "I apologize if earlier I upset you with the story, I told you."

She looked taken a back.

"No, my lord you didn't upset me. I was just lost in thought. Taking in your story. I just feel so bad for the demon."

"Excuse me?" Count Alejandro did not expect those words to come out of her mouth. Though he was annoyed at how she called him, my lord'.

"I mean, Rosa could have just told the demon she didn't love him. But instead, she sent him away.

All those years the demon thought she might have had feelings for him, especially if he brought back the rose.

I always adored Rosa, I thought she was this kind girl that would love the demon. But no, she was just some shallow girl who couldn't see past the demon's appearance and give him a chance." She looked genuinely sad.

"But I wonder if a demon pronounced his love to you would you give him a chance?" he asked, his voice reflecting his seriousness.

"Of course. Though, I'm sure it won't matter soon because I'll be married to Bartello." Count Alejandro stiffened. "You don't like him, do you?" she said.

"No, I have no problem with him, I only worry about why he'd propose to you so suddenly and send you into a strangers house to prove…well I don't know why he sent you here."

"Well, he didn't say I had to steal one of your roses, just a blue rose. You happened to be the first person who I thought of who owned one."

"That's slightly cliché." He chuckled.

"Yeah, just a bit." She smiled. A maid, she was a young girl, walked in then and said,

"I apologize my lord, to disturb you, but a gentleman has come calling."

"Oh?" said Count Alejandro.

"Yes, he said his name was Bartello Mevidue." The maid said. Both Count Alejandro and Carina froze in shock.

Carina stood up, followed by the count. They followed the maid to the entry. There stood an extremely handsome man.

He had short blond hair and wore clothes that flaunted his wealth. He looked at Carina and his brown eyes lit up, he ran to her and embraced her.

"Carina! Thank God you're alright! I've looked for you everywhere. What were you thinking?" he looked at her, giving her a stern look, "When I said I'd like a blue rose instead of a ring, I didn't mean for you to go out and try to steal one.

I'm flattered at your dedication though.

"Count Alejandro I'm eternally grateful for your kindness to my Carina." She flinched at the inflection.

"No, it was my pleasure." Count Alejandro replied, "His voice had a monotone like quality to it. Carina looked over to him, his face was blank. For some reason her heart sank.

"Yes, thank you." Carina said, her voice matching his.

"Come, come Carina we have wedding plans to make. Oh, and please forget about the blue rose. I have you and that's all I need." He smiled and pulled her towards the door.

"Goodbye then." She called back to Count Alejandro.

"I wish you happiness." He said. Carina's eyes widened, she gave a weak smile and followed Bartello.

When the door shut, Count Alejandro continued to stare at the door.

"So that's it? You just let her go?" Ellen said from atop the stairs.

"Yes. He'll take care of her."

"But she even said-" Count Alejandro cut her off.

"If she really was put in that situation, I doubt she would do as she said she would.

I want all the servants left dismissed, until the moon has returned. Now leave me." His voice quavered.

"But my lord-"

"LEAVE ME!" he bellowed. Ellen flinched but hurried away. Count Alejandro walked down to the basement, into the room made for him.

He locked the door behind him, closed his eyes and let the darkness have him.

One of Bartello's maids led Carina to her room. It was huge, with a canopy bed and a walk-in closet. The closet had only a few dresses in it, but the maid assured her that they'd be going to a dress shop to have some custom made. But that was not something Carina was looking forward to doing.

Carina looked around the extravagant room, it all looked very expensive, and sighed. She didn't want the wealth she wanted…she wanted…she knew what she wanted but it shocked her.

How selfish could she get? She had all this, yet she wanted something else. A knock came from the door, interrupting Carina's fretting.

"Come in." she called. Bartello walked into her room, wearing a smile that looked a little strained.

"Listen Carina I'm sorry but business calls so I'll be away for a few months. We'll have the wedding sometime then."

"Where are you going?" Carina asked.

"That's nothing for you to worry your pretty little head about." He pats her on the head.

"I could go with you." Carina suggested.

"Love, if we're going to be married then you'd better get a couple things straight. I go on business trips a lot and you are staying here.

That's how it will work." He sounded as if he thought she was mentally challenged.

"Alright, I understand." But really, she didn't, Carina bowed her head so he wouldn't be insulted by her outburst.

"It's okay love, you'll get used to how I run things." He lifted her chin and kissed her. To Carina, it felt wrong.

Bartello pulled away and smiled, he left the room leaving Carina in a daze. She didn't want this, but it was the best she would ever get. A tear trickled down her face, she wished for someone, someone who didn't love her back.

Carina looked up at Count Alejandro's mansion the next night. Bartello was already away, and the maids wouldn't be up in either his mansion, No one would know she was here, neither Bartello.

Carina found the window to her room, wearing her black pants and sweatshirt that the maid and returned to her earlier that day.

She scaled the wall, she had done it once before, and opened the window. Carina chose her room because it was probably the only window unlocked.

Luckily, it was. She climbed in and headed for the door, pressing her ear to it to make sure it was quiet outside of it.

She sneaked out of the room and down the hall, slipped down the stairs and turned right.

Carina walked down the familiar hall to a large oak door. She opened the door to the courtyard she loved. It was dark but that didn't stop Carina, she went straight for the roses.

Carina knew living with Bartello would leave her unhappy for the rest of her life. She wanted one last thing to give her joy, the rose. She leaned over and plucked one from the bush, holding it close to her chest.

A shadow seemed to descend upon Carina, she looked behind her and her entire being froze. A dark figure loomed near the wall, something about it made her skin crawl.

"Why are you here?" the dark figure hissed, but somehow it sounded familiar.

"I'm sorry, I just wanted a rose." She said, her voice almost a whisper. The figure chuckled darkly and said,

"Well, well, well, I feel as if we've done this before." The figure walked out of the shadows and Carina's breath caught in her throat.

It had skin that was pitch black and even under the hood the figure wore, Carina could see horns the length of fingers curled towards each other. Its actual fingers were long and slender that ended in slightly curled talons. But on the figures back were huge closed, black wings. But the figures face,

"Count Alejandro?" His face still looked very similar.

"Yes, I'm surprised you could tell." His voice had taken on a mocking tone.

"But…how?" she stammered.

"How? I'm a demon," he smiled, and Carina saw his eye teeth were long and sharp. He continued, "My grandfather was the demon who fell in love with Rosa."

"Then the story…"

"Yes, the story was true. You'd think I would have learned from it. My father did, he married another demon girl. But me, I did the same as my grandfather. I had to fall in love with a human." Carina blinked, shocked by his words.

"Are you…are you saying you…love me?" She looked into his eyes and immediately felt calm.

Alejandro's face shone with anguish until he turned his face away from her, so she could not see it.

"Yes," his voice came out in a whisper, "I do." Carina felt a smile on her lips. She knew she should be scared out of her mind, and running away screaming but she couldn't see a reason why. She was frightened, a little, but she didn't want to run, away at least.

"Why are you smiling? Let me guess, you've come up a clever idea to get rid of me? What is it this time? A purple rose? Or maybe polka dot?" he sneered. Carina flinched at his harsh tone. She looked at the rose in her hands and said,

"No, this one will be fine."

"Excuse me?"

"I don't need anything."

"Oh? And what about Bartello?" his took on a mocking tone.

"I can't marry him because I don't love him. I thought I could reconcile my happiness, to save my life. But I can't do it.

Up until about a week ago, my life was pretty much pointless. I didn't have a reason to live. But then I got a taste of real happiness and I fell in love. But I thought my feelings were one sided. So, I left." Alejandro stared at her stunned.

"Now I know your lying. Maybe you did have feelings for me but there is no way you still can. Not after you've found out what I am."

"I don't care what you are." She said lifting her chin defiantly.

"You really expect me to believe that?" he almost shouted. Carina reflexively flinched.

"Ow!" she looked at the rose still in hand. Numerous little drops of blood started to bead on her hand.

Carina reached into her pocket and retrieved a white handkerchief that Bartello had given her.

She tried to tie it around her hand but with one hand and holding a rose it was impossible. Count Alejandro sighed and said, "You're hopeless."

He shook his head and reached for the handkerchief. Carina flinched slightly as he did. But he grabbed the cloth and swiftly tied it around her hand. He then took the rose from her other hand and broke off all the thorns.

Carina laughed and said, "Thank you." She reached out to take it but he held up his hand to stop her. Carina gave him a curious look, wondering if he planned on sending her back to Bartello's without it.

He carefully slipped the rose behind her ear. He started to draw his hand away, but Carina held it to her cheek.

"This always calmed me." She breathed. Count Alejandro was torn, he wanted so much to believe her, but he didn't want to give in only to have her turn around and say she didn't really care for him.

"I don't understand, how can you stand there and say you love me when I look like this?"

"Because it wasn't just your looks that I love, and you really don't look that horrible now," and he didn't, to Carina, after she got over the initial shock of seeing him.

He was still handsome, in a gothic sort of way, "Though it certainly didn't hinder my feelings, but I fell in love with this," she put her hand where his heart was.

Count Alejandro flinched at her touch. But she just smiled. He slipped his other hand around her waist and pulled her into his chest. She sighed in content and put her arms under his.

Carina looked up at Alejandro's face. She reached up her hands and pushed back his hood. He still had his dark hair and even darker eyes. They still held apprehension; she could tell he wanted to believe her though. She tried to think how she could make him see that she wasn't lying.

So, she pressed her lips to his, wrapping her arms around his neck, holding him there.

At that moment she didn't care if he was demon, human, vampire, or an elf. Alejandro's mind went blank, he thought he was pushing it when he held her, that that would frighten her enough.

Carina had kissed him. She was kissing him, even though he looked like something that belonged in a nightmare. But all rational thoughts seemed to fly out of his head, and he kissed her back.

Suddenly Alejandro felt his body shudder and quiver. He pulled away from Carina as his vision swam.

Just as suddenly, it stopped, he looked at his now human hands. He was in his human form. He didn't understand how, the sun was still down and would be for many more hours.

"Well, it's about time!" said a voice from the doorway to the courtyard. Both Carina and Alejandro turned to see Ellen standing there.

"Ellen?" said Alejandro.

"Of course? Who else would I be? And didn't I tell you that Alejandro loved you?"

"You did." She smiled at looked at Alejandro who smiled in return. But then something occurred to her. "But I still don't understand the connection between the noises during the new moon and his feelings for me." Carina questioned.

"When I change into my true form, my demon form, it's a little more violent during a new moon. I'm sorry if I scared you." He said contrite.

"That was you?" Carina asked him.

"Yes, I'm sorry." He apologized, giving her look that made her heart break.

"It's all right, really." said Carina. She gave him a smile that made him forget what they were talking about.

"Though speaking of changing, you wouldn't happen to know why I've changed into my human form?" Alejandro asked Ellen.

"Of course, I do. I am the reason you can appear human at all."

"What?" he asked confused.

"The sorceress, who gave your grandfather the ability to transform into a human until midnight and let the spell pass on to his children, that was me.

I'm not powerful enough to let you appear human after midnight, that's when a demon's at its strongest." Ellen said.

"That doesn't explain why I'm human now."

"You aren't human, dear, but the only thing allowing you to overcome your demonic strength and amplify my magic is that girl in your arms." Alejandro's eyes grew wide.

"Me?" Carina was amazed.

"Who else would it be? Part of my spell was that if the demon in question could find a girl to love with all his heart and truly love him back then he could remain in his human form whenever he wanted to.

You can change back into your true form whenever you want, of course.

"But you aren't human, that is beyond my power. I doubt anyone can accomplish that except for an extremely powerful demon, one that can wield magic."

"Carina," Alejandro turned to her, "I'm not human, and I doubt I ever will be. Unless, you wish for me to be, then I will seek out a being powerful enough to make it so."

"NO! I forbid you to leave me in search for something that doesn't even matter to me!" Carina snapped, "I finally have you, I'm not letting you go so easily.

Alejandro smiled at her, feeling so happy he could burst. Instead, he pressed his lips to hers. Reveling in the feeling of loving and being loved in return. Alejandro pulled away, only to press his lips to her forehead.

"Don't worry, I'm not going anywhere." He reassured her.

"Promise?"

"I promise." He smiled and turned to where Ellen was, "Thank you" but he stopped when he saw Ellen was no longer there. "She'll turn up soon enough." Alejandro turned back to her and said,

"I want to give you something." He whispered in her ear.

"Okay." She replied.

"I'll have to change into my demon form though, is that okay?"

"Of course." Alejandro smiled and stepped away from Carina and unlocked the magic that held him in a strange form.

A rippling sensation went through him, and he felt his form shift and twist until he was his version of normal. Alejandro looked over at Carina to see she had a worried look on her face.

"What's wrong?" he asked her, anxious that she decided he was too monstrous for her to love.

"You said it hurt when you change," she reached for his arm, holding it close to her, "Are you okay? Alejandro laughed lightly.

"I'm alright, I don't think it'll be as painful anymore."

"Good."

"I'll be right back." He said, but she didn't release his arm.

"Can I come with you?" she asked. "Please?" she added after he gave her an apprehensive look.

"Okay but I hope you're alright with flying." He spread out his wings to show what he meant. Carina's face lit up as she thought of it. "Come on." He scooped her up onto his arms and jumped off the ground into the air. Carina clung to Alejandro, the smile still on her face.

He flew over the top of the mansion until he came to another courtyard. But this one was different, it was overgrown and only one color, blue. He landed in a spot where the flowers hadn't taken over.

He set her on the ground and transformed back into his human form. Carina had walked over to one of the vines,

"Blue roses" she breathed.

"The same ones my grandfather created by crying for the death of the woman he loved. We had to fly because there is no door, the mansion was built around it." He reached over and took one. Alejandro snapped off all the thorns and turned to her.

"Carina, will you marry me?" he asked, his voice soft. Shocked, Carina froze, a blush coated her cheeks.

"Yes," she whispered, "Yes! Of course, I'll marry you." The smile he gave her was breathtaking. He slipped the red rose out from behind her ear and put the blue rose in its stead. He pressed his lips to hers, and Carina wrapped her arms around his neck.

"I love you." She said.

"Do you think you can give happiness a chance?"

"Happiness? I expect much more than that." She smiled.

"Good, because we'll have much more than just that. Want to go for another fly?" Carina nodded eagerly.

Alejandro's change was swifter this time, he leapt into the air with Carina in his arms. His wings carried him and Carina towards the new moon. She was smiling, the rose still in her hair.

The symbol of his love and her returning it. She pressed her lips to his. He was overjoyed, no matter what form he took she would love him, and he would always love her. Carina was his true love….

Chapter 31

Midnight Dance

The stars were shining above us. Each dazzling star was a light on a disco ball that Angel and I danced under. The night was dressed in inky black to match my clothes.

Angel and I change direction in and out of the trees to our own beat. Grass was the perfect dance floor. The softness of it cushioned our steps.

Nature was all the music we needed. The chilling wind was our pipes, seedpods were our maracas, and the pecking of a bird was our drum. The leaves so high on the trees were swaying with us in the wind. This part of the world seemed meant for us.

How long could this last? A second, a minute, an hour, a day, a lifetime? The crisp air held no answer for us.

We just kept weaving back and forth in each other's arms. Time was not our problem. Nor was hate, envy or competition. The world for that moment was perfect and could never be duplicated.

Angel and I were spinning around a rose bush when I heard a crack of a gun and Angel went limp. I was so confused I didn't know what was happening.

Angel's body fell to the ground as I dropped next to him. Blood was seeping through his shirt like a raging river.

My salty tears mixed with his blood as I sat there gazing into his glassy blue eyes. I laid my head on his chest sobbing when the police sirens could be heard in the distance.

The sirens were getting closer and closer and soon they could be heard right ahead of us. I lifted my tear-streaked face to meet the officer when I heard a faint sound. I turned my head towards Angel and then I realized his pale lips were moving.

I fell to my knees at his side listening. Barely louder than coo of a dove he whispered, " Remember me, Alice. Remember me and our midnight dance." Then Angel left the world. He left me. He left an unfinished dance that could have lasted a lifetime.

Chapter 32

The Rocks

Everything was just right. The ocean waves gently tapping the shore, the cloudless sky, the booming, distant music carried by the restless breeze through the trees.

Serenity filled my heart-broken body as I gazed into his welcoming eyes. I lay there for a while; we said nothing.

Then again, nothing really needed to be said. Everything was already known. This was foreign to me, a subconscious knowing; a beautiful, unspoken unity.

I could feel it deep off the very rock we were sitting on. We were no longer two strangers tossed together, uncertain of what we were searching for or why we were there in that moment sitting together.

Both of us did know that we had found something that no one else could understand.

The throbbing in my heart eased as he wrapped his arms around me. I was finally at peace. Although I was dizzy from looking through the kaleidoscope of my emotions, his comforting touch soothed me.

I inhaled the sweet lake air and sighed, my body relaxing into his.

Chicago's skyline danced in the distance while boats played in the seemingly endless, but conquerable Lake Michigan.

Everything faded while I was with him, like the blurring edges of an old photograph. It was just us together on the rocks.

Nothing else mattered. Not the huge crowds of confused college students surrounding us, not the blaring rock music, not the anxious police, not the girls screaming and laughing in the water next to us, not the neighboring couples on rocks, not the birds circling nearby. Nothing.

The whirlwind of life stopped for those few moments, and in those few moments I realized what life is about.

It's about the unexpected when you can escape, and you discover something that you'd never think you'd find.

Maybe it's impossible to describe and fully understand exactly what I felt and found that day on those rocks, but every time I look into his eyes.

I returned to that moment of serenity and the burdens of life were lifted off my shoulders.

It is a pure and raw connection, a rare harmony I found among the peace of life. In recollection, I feel fortunate to have experienced such a moment.

It was just Willie and me and the rocks. I hope to have many more.

Chapter 33

The Complex Word

Marriage is such a complex word that cannot be described in one or two phrases…

Let's just say that marriage is the sacrament shared by people of all ages, cultures, and countries; this sacred bond performed by two loving souls will sculpt the rest of their lives, for better or for worse.

Marriage should not be based on convenience or lust, but appreciation and determination.

Marriage, the blooming flower of love, comes when two people have fallen in love and are willing to make any necessary sacrifices to remain eternally enamored.

Sacrifices that may be hard and internally painful for a few short moments, but completely worthwhile in the long run.

The flower of marriage gradually blossoms as two individuals share their lives together and beautify peacefully throughout their elder years. Every flower loses a petal every-so-often, as every couple face downfall periodically.

Marriage is a person informing their special someone that they are willing to lose a petal or two, but that they will never let the marriage shrivel up and die.

Both spouses vow to remain faithful and stay strong when life throws unexpected curve balls towards them. Overcoming the curve balls is like watering a flower, they allow the couple to grow stronger and grow closer.

During matrimony, the couple not only makes promises to themselves, but to each other as well.

The vow "for better, for worse" promises that both people in the relationship will accept one another no matter how stressful and unsightly situations may become.

As every flower has its off seasons when it is not in bloom and does not comply with the weather, every couple face hardship and heartache throughout their journey through life.

However, the offseason only intensifies the flowers magnificence as the rough times only make the happy times more enjoyable with a couple.

Marriage is a promise that two spouses will never give up, even when they get hit with some harsh winds.

The next four words "for richer, for poor" are a promise that money will not make or break the relationship. This vow is a guarantee that lust will never be placed above love and that each spouse will continue loving the other if money becomes tight.

Maybe the flower doesn't look so attractive in the winter months, when most of the precious petals have shriveled and fallen to the cold ground and the aged leaves are turning from an eccentric green to a pale yellow.

This change in appearance doesn't take away the inner beauty of the flower. The same concept is applicable when I say that a man is no less of a man once he's been laid off from his high-paying job and must begin working as a waiter in the fast-food industry.

Love comes from the heart and soul, not from the wallet. The last of the vows, "until death do us part," are crucial to the meaning of marriage.

This firm, meaningful words let, not only the couple, but everyone know that the two souls reciting the words promise to cherish each other for the rest of their lives.

This means that twenty years down the road, when the husband has begun to grow more hair on his back and less on his head and the wife's eyes no longer sparkle in the light, but rather droop and sag through the passing days, the couple will still be just as in love as when they were first married.

The matrimonial flower has continued to grow over time and is now just a beautiful as an ever-lasting marriage.

I have no intention of enforcing a strict and limited definition of marriage; my intention is simply to introduce society to a new point of view on marriage and perhaps influence the minds of young souls throughout the world that may be grasping the concept of marriage a little too lightly.

Embrace the marriage and accept it for its imperfections.

Chapter 34

The Wish

It started out with a simple excuse.

"You forgot my birthday!" she said to Paul. It wasn't a true disappointment. Annie knew he didn't know. That didn't stop her from guilt-tripping him.

"Well…what can I do to make it up to you?" he asked.

"Oh, please don't look at me with those eyes!" she thought to herself as she melted inside.

"A cookie!" she said smiling. "That isn't peanut butter or oatmeal!" she added.

"Ok then" he said. "I'll see you later" he watched her get off the bus.

He put his head back and continued to listen to crappy music on his iPod.

She walked home trying to be discreet while she watched the bus fade out. She sighed.

At that time and place she wanted him and no one else.

The doorbell rang!!!! Her heart skipped a beat…her stomach churning "He's here!!!" she thought to herself.

"Hey!" she said cheerfully, opening the door.

"I brought you your cookies!" Paul said with a smirk.

"Pooh!" she replied in an awkward high pitched hyper voice. She took the cookies and giggled while she put them in the kitchen.

"Hey! Let's go get slushies!" she said, grabbing his hand as they fled from her house.

His hand touched hers as they walked. She wanted to feel their fingers tangled together desperately.

"Don't touch me!" she exclaimed. "If the neighbors drive by, I'm dead" she giggled.

They walked passed cornfields and barns and made it to the slushier place. They sat at a picnic table and ate their slushiest.

"Hey…let's go a different way on the way back!!" Annie exclaimed gesturing towards a cornfield.

"I can't believe I'm walking through a cornfield with you!!!"

"Yes, but all my neighbors drive by on the road" she said talking his hand. She heard a sound that may have been an animal. "EEEEKKKK!!!!" she squealed, jumping towards him.

"I've got you" he whispered.

"I hope so" she replied giggling.

"It is time for your birthday present," he said smirking.

She thought it was going to happen then and there. It didn't. They made their way to the creek.

"Ok…this isn't going to work" she said turning around.

"All we have to do is jump" he said jumping across the creek. "You can do it" he looked at her.

She jumped and fell on top of him. "Hey there" she said giggling.

She rolled on top of him. "Want to make out?" he asked at an attempt to sound cocky.

"NO!" She pushed him off. "We have to go through the creek" she walked into the water that came up to her ankles. Sneakers and all…she didn't care if she got wet.

"You're crazy!" he laughed.

"Oh no!" she thought to herself. "He's looking at me with those eyes again".

He bent down to roll his pants up. She wanted him.

Now, she knew that she wasn't going home without kissing him.

She walked to him and quickly threw her arms around his neck. "Hi" she said cheerfully.

"Hi?" he responded with confusion.

Their lips met. Her head was spinning. Never in a million years would she expect herself to be kissing him.

This was exactly what she wanted. She pulled away. He was looking at her with 'those eyes' again.

It was enough to send her over the edge. Before she could even say anything, he kissed her once again. She'd never thought the perfect kiss really existed….until now. She pulled away and looked at him. He'd just wasted his first kiss on her.

Chapter 35

The Big Confusion

I watch her as she flirts with other guys. It breaks my heart. Every now and then she catches me watching.

She gets this confused look on her face. I hope I confuse her as much as she confuses me.

She waves at me with a smile on her face. I pull on the mask once again and walk over.

The once confidante guy shrinks away.

It sucks not being able to talk to your best friend.

Chapter 36

The Bracelet

The sun was finally rising. I was there to watch. The bloody red faded into pink; the pink faded to orange.

Usually something as beautiful as this would be amazing to me, but today I just stared blankly out my window.

It's over, even before I can fully wake up my mind is filled with thoughts, it's over. I'll never be held in his strong arms again.

Never feel his warm lips pressed against mine. Never hear him whisper "I love you, so many things I'll miss.

So many memories I hold that are going to burden me. I'm not sure yet whether to regret it all or not. He's the reason I know love. He's the reason for the smile on my face the last few months.

Yet, he's the reason I can't even look at myself in the mirror. He's the reason I lay here watching such wonderful things with lifeless eyes. I'm not sure how to feel, and this is just the very beginning of the day.

My fingers meet my neck as if by instinct to find his necklace. The beloved Virgin Mary I've been carrying around since that cold November day.

The little piece of him I carried with me always, as if to show I was his, or was his. The words hurt even in my mind. Feeling around my skin for it I remember the anger I had had last night and crawled out of bed. I remember ripping it off me and throwing it across the room.

In the faint sunlight I see the little silver piece of metal glinting in the corner next to my dresser.

I retrieve it and feeling the cold texture beneath my fingers triggers a hundred memories at once.

He and I together in the woods, sneaking kisses as we threw leaves at each other. Once I got caught in my hair.

As he gently took it out, he kissed my forehead. Then slowly my cheek, down to my neck, then finally right on the Virgin Mary.

After that memory flew by the one of him handing me the necklace came to mind. He had put it on me himself and whispered, "You're not allowed to ever take it off. You're mine always."

I clamp my eyes shut and curl up in a ball right on the floor. There's nowhere I can hide when I close my eyes he's there.

He and that beautiful face, beautiful smile, everything. I'm not sure how much a heart can take before it literally breaks but mine aches so badly.

I think I'm going to be sick. I pull myself tighter, gripping onto my legs. The rough rope tying the necklace together digs into my clenched fist. There's nothing left to do but cry, so I do.

I'm not sure when the tears stopped but I didn't hear my family moving around downstairs so it must still be early.

Slowly I lift myself from the floor and lifelessly dress myself. I'm not even sure what I put on; I don't even care anymore.

All I know is that I want to go outside. Now. I can't have this with me anymore. I told him he could have it back, why should I keep it with me?

I silently make my way downstairs and open the door. I don't feel myself doing any of these things, but I must be because I'm suddenly outside standing in the middle of the road.

No cars pass by, no neighbor cat's meow, not even a car alarm in the distance. It must be around five a.m. and I am completely alone.

I am just staring away to nowhere. I fell to my knees on the wet ground; it must have rained last night.

I could care less. Unclenching my hand, I watch the necklace fall to the ground. I need to realize it's not a part of me anymore.

It's just a piece of jewelry sitting in the middle of the road. It doesn't hold the memories, I do.

Behind me is the sound of running feet. Pit, pat, pit, pat. He was always a fast runner, light on his feet.

They gradually slow as they grow closer. As he realizes there's a girl in the middle of the road, one who probably looks like a mess right now.

One who's heart is completely broken. I look up and feel as if a dagger were just thrust at me.

It just seems so wrong to see him standing there in front of me, a picture of perfection. Even from here I can see his dark eyes, I can imagine the emerald, green lines flashing.

What an evil twist of fate that we show up here at the same time.

To my surprise he doesn't turn and runs in the other direction.

Instead, he walks toward me and falls beside me. I can hear his deep breaths and possibly even tears.

"I understand if you can't believe me or don't want to hear it, but I am truly sorry."

The sound of his voice is like poison.

"You're right," I say and stand up. "I don't want to hear it. It kills me to not have you, but you know what, if you'd really cared you would have never done anything to hurt me."

"People make mistakes," he mumbled.

"Yeah, they do Carlos, but everything you've said, wasn't a mistake. It was reality, and if that's who you really are I don't want you anymore.

Sorry doesn't change a thing, it wasn't exactly sorry you were saying when you were breaking my heart."

I kicked the necklace at his knees and turned and walked away. My hands shook, my head was spinning.

My stomach stumbled but there was something inside of me that kept me going. Kept me from doing the easy thing and jumping into his arms, forgiving him for all his wrongs.

Someone stronger inside of me knew that the pain would end, a new day would begin.

Something greater would come along one day. Plus, there was something oh so satisfying about leaving him alone in the middle of the street.

I think tonight I'll pray for his misery. I wonder if it'd be wrong to be that selfish. Oh well, not like I was ever that religious in the first place.

Here I am again making my way to the train tracks, my sanctuary. I remember wishing I could leave this town and find new places to go, but right now no other place could make me feel better.

No other place would feel like home. I cut through my little dirty path on the side of the road and I'm there.

Almost feeling as though I'm back to normal. I balance on the hard outer railing, feeling as though I'm back to the beginning of summer. I know I'm going to be okay.

Chapter 37

A Love Story

As I was walking down the hall where the sophomore lockers were. I bumped into Nilsa.

Everyone knew her and everyone hated her. She butted into everyone's conversation. Everywhere you where she was there .

Just sitting there staring at you, listening to every bit of the conversation. Nilsa was known as the 'Stalker' because of her ability to follow you around when you didn't want her.

If you talked about her and she found out, she would run to her mother and cry about it until her mom called the school.

But normally the school did nothing about it. The whole entire county hated the family; they were just too creepy and too obnoxious.

After I said I was sorry, she initially started a long and boring conversation which was more like a speech about her mom letting her finally get a kitten.

I was so bored and wanted to leave but I couldn't because she would cry if I just walked away.

It was too early to think of a way to say goodbye nicely. As I was standing there patiently listening, Ray turned around the corner. He saw the look of desperation mixed with boredom on my face and said," Hey Nina, Mr. P. wants to see A.S.A.P."

"Okay I'll get right on it, thanks," I replied.

I ran towards my locker and breathed a sigh of relief when Ray caught up with me. "Thanks for saving me that was the worst thing in the world." I told him.

"No problem, when I see a beautiful girl in distress, I immediately break out my shining armor."

"I thank you very much Sir Lancelot... although that line was pretty cheesy."

"So, what are you doing tonight?'" He asked in an innocent voice as if he was clueless.

I played along, "Uh... I don't know... maybe play in my basketball game and then rush to get to the school dance.

"Oh... sounds interesting. So, I was wondering if your dad could drive me to the game and then maybe give me another lift to the dance."

"I don't see why he couldn't. Don't forget that my game is at 6:30 though."

"I won't. So, I will see you at lunch, alright."

"Alright, see you later."

The bell rang and I ran to first block which is Spanish today for me. I got in the classroom just in time and was reluctant to see Liz sitting in the back with a seat with my name on it.

"Hey," she said with a big smile on her face. I sat down, then the teacher, Mrs. Chaqueta walked in and sat down. She grabbed a piece of paper, scribbled something, and then took attendance.

When she was finished, she said, "You are going to have a project due when you come back from break."

Chapter 38

We are Meant for each Other

I stand here hopelessly, with nothing but confusion in my eyes and a dandelion held tight in between my hands.

I stare at you from a distance, thinking, "We were meant to be", although it, as what I'm seeing now, can never happen.

I remember in kindergarten, when we first met on the playground, you would push me on the swings so that I could finally touch the skies and feel the wind in my hair, like I always wanted to do on my own.

When I told you to go away, you carelessly ran behind me, disappearing from my life.

Within 5 minutes, you returned with a freshly picked yellow dandelion in your hand. You reached it out to me with a wide smile and said, "We were meant to be."

I remember in fifth grade, after you followed me home from school, you rode your bike passed my house waving crazily at me.

Annoyed, I turned around and entered the door. Within 5 minutes, you came back to my house, ringing the doorbell rapidly until I answered.

"I can't find my way home, " you said with an innocent look. After I helped you locate your house, you faced me closely.

With a wide smile, you said, "We were meant to be," and gazed around the grass, looking for something that I couldn't quite determine.

"What are you looking for?" I blurted out as you began to kneel and scurry the grass. You got up, brushing away the dirt on your jeans and ran into the house.

I watched, through the screen door, as you charged out the back side of your house, reaching down to pluck a dandelion from the ground.

You came back out the front, reaching it out to me and repeated, "We were meant to be."

I remember in eighth grade, after you had found where my locker was, you slipped a bright yellow note into it.

I watched you from down the hall and decided to scare you away. When I darted up to you, yelling, you ran away, just like you did in kindergarten when I told you to leave.

I hurriedly opened my locker, curious to see what the note said, "We were meant to be."

After 5 minutes of ripping the note into pieces, you showed up behind me with a bright yellow dandelion in your hand.

You reached it out to me with a wide smile and said, "We were meant to be."

I remember last week, when I introduced you to my boyfriend, you followed us the whole day at the mall.

You vanished after we sat down for lunch. But within 5 minutes, you returned with a handful of freshly picked dandelions, and with words and a smile that I knew so well, you repeated for the last time, "We were meant to be."

As I took the cluster of flowers and carelessly threw them to the floor, I watched the last remains of you vanish through the exit that led into millions of different directions.

Now, however, I stand here at this very moment, with nothing but confusion in my eyes and a dandelion held tight in between my hands.

In regret, I gaze at you and your new girlfriend, sharing a smile, a laugh, and dandelion.

I stare at you from a distance, thinking, "We were meant to be", although it, as what I'm seeing now, can never happen.

Chapter 39

Our Story

She sees now that nothing had ever been fake. From the glances that had started their relationship to the kisses that had consumed it in the later portion.

Everything had gone all right not shortly after. Whether she wanted to remember or not, she could still feel his lips on her skin, hear him whispering in her ear, still smell him on the cardigan she had borrowed and never gave back.

The feeling of longing makes its course in her body each time she sees him. From seeing him in the courtyard each morning, to catching a glimpse of him running to class, the feeling of longing just bursts open and tears her heart out along with it.

Half the time, she wants to go after him, once she almost did. She wants to run up to him, grab him and tell him how much she wants him, how much she needs him, how nothing has changed her feelings for him.

But she can't. Because she cares about him. Because his future doesn't need a flighty mischievous girlfriend.

Each day he wonders, 'Does she still care?' But he never knows. He doesn't want to admit to himself, but he misses her. He misses her laugh, her smile, her eyes.

He misses waking up in the morning and finding her fast asleep and clutching her teddy bear beside him. He misses everything.

Not that he would admit it or anything, he couldn't. He had buried the part of him that had included her, deep into his heart. It would cause him too much heartbreak to dig it back up again.

He sees her often. He feels her eyes trained on him whilst he sits in the courtyard, tapping his notebook with a pen, trying to think of something to write.

He hears the whispers and the rumors that swirl around, almost dangerously. But he doesn't listen.

Not even when he hears the words, "Carl likes Karen again? Ew." Because there is no possible way that she would love him again, he was sure of it.

She talks in her sleep. She knows because he's told her every time, she woke up beside him.

So, when her mom goes up to her and tells her that she's been mumbling in her sleep about elevators, she's not surprised.

Ever since that day, she's wanted nothing more than to go back and hold the elevator doors open to ask him, "Why are you giving up on us? Fight for me."

Unfortunately, she doesn't have that power, she will never have that power. All she can do is hope that he notices her staring at him each day.

Nightmares. He's never been a big fan of them, but he always has them. From the disastrous T-Ball event, to breaking up with the love of his life.

He has them, but no one knows. It's always the same one. The blackout that occurred in the elevator keeps replaying and replaying in his dreams, stealing his breath, and making him wish for a time machine.

According to a very well-known scientist, time is relative. He's never actually experienced that until the day she accidentally slams into him, causing their books to fly.

Dropping down to pick them up, he tries to use the moment in time to his advantage. He wants time to slow down, so they can talk. But when he looks up, she's gone. Time is relative. That suck.

She had his notebook. From the day she had slammed into him. She must have accidentally scooped it up with her own.

Staring at the cover of the small leather notebook, she gets an image of him writing in it.

It was the night on the beach, the night of the White Party. He was writing about her. She didn't need to read it to tell. His eyes would tell her. They spoke to her in ways no one would ever understand.

Shaking fingers, she opened the notebook, the pages crinkling as she did so. She traced the outline of his name written at the top.

She sat down and began to read. Stories burst out at her, feeding her imagination. The stories had one constant.

Each time she read them, hot tears flowed gently and quietly down her cheeks. He loved her, but it was too late now.

"I miss her." It's the first time he's said it aloud. But no one's around to hear it. So, he decides to transform it into writing.

Searching his bag repeatedly, he can't find his notebook. Giving up, he resorts to his laptop.

Luckily, someone probably found it and tossed it. But a part of him can't help but wonder what if someone had shown it to her.

Wouldn't she then see that he still loved her? That he wanted nothing more than to get back together with her. Shaking the thoughts from his head, he starts to write.

The more she reads, the more she doubts. Her mind is clouded with the thought that she might just be some writing material and everything he wrote was worthless.

She won't know unless she asks him and there is no way she's doing that. Instead, she hugs the notebook to her chest, pretending its him and re-reading it every night so that her tears can lull her to sleep.

After two weeks of keeping it, something in her mind tells her to return it to him. She doesn't want to, of course, but she can't let go of him without giving it back.

So, she sneaks to the loft one early Sunday morning when he usually sleeps in. She greets Rufus with sad eyes.

One glance at the notebook and cardigan in her hands, and he knows what she's here to do.

She snuck into his room and placed his notebook and cardigan on his desk. She hopes he finds the note she hid in the small leather notebook.

Turning to leave, she catches sight of him. He's sleeping contentedly, rolled over on his side and slightly snoring. She creeps closer to him.

She hadn't been this close to him in months, not including the day they ran into each other.

Leaning down, she puts a hand on his cheek, kissing him on the forehead. I love you. She whispers before turning and leaving, tears dripping down her face.

She runs out, hair flying behind her. "I miss you." She whispers as the elevator makes its slow descent down. She wishes he was there, arms wrapped tightly around her, kissing her.

She had been here, in his room. Returning his notebook and cardigan. He could smell the familiar scent that she wore every day and he had heard her before she left.

He wasn't sure if what he had heard was an illusion though. They were over, weren't they? But if they were, why was she here personally? It confused his mind, her very presence did that to him anyway. If she loved him, wouldn't she have stayed?

He continues meditating until noon when he finally decides to pick up the notebook and write for the first time in two weeks.

Flipping to an empty page, a note fell out and into his lap. Picking it up with unsteady fingers, he opens it. I miss you. I love you. I'm sorry. It reads in her messy handwriting.

He walks towards her the next day, wondering where he got the courage to do this. He silently hands her the note, his face impassive. A million thoughts run through his mind as he does so.

Rejection washes through her face as he stands there, waiting. "Open it." He says. Biting her lip, she shakes her head.

"No." She watches as his brow wrinkled; lips cast downward in a frown. Please. It's not much of a plea but one look at his warm brown eyes does it for her. She opens the paper, her hands barely past shaking.

The crinkling sound of it opening makes him lower his head from her eyes to the paper.

She slowly lifts the paper up and reads what she had written yesterday. Hurt oozes from her every pore. Why are you mocking me? Her eyes seem to say.

He shakes his head again. Keep reading. He says, tapping the paper softly and taking a step closer to her. Her green eyes focus on him briefly before turning back to the paper.

He watches her every movement as she reads the paper. Her eyes scan the words he had written last night, before looking up at him and darting back to the paper.

She mouths the words, and without prompt, he says the same words out loud. "I'm still in love with you. I'm sorry that I took so long. Please forgive me."

She moves in towards him. "Do you mean it?" She asks, her eyes cautious and hesitant. He nods slowly.

"Every single word. Do you?" She nods and suddenly finds herself pressed against him, wrapped in a big warm hug. "I've missed you." He whispers in her ear. "I've missed you too. For the longest time." She whispers back. That was all he needed to press his lips to hers, sealing their future together.

Chapter 40

Cherry Flavored Kisses

"I'll call you later," Davie told me after school.

"Okay," I lightly smiled as I turned towards my locker. Davie touched my shoulder and spun me around, grabbing both my hands in his.

I looked up at his soft, green eyes as he pulled me close to him and kissed me on my forehead.

"What was that for ?" I laughed. I could tell I was blushing.

"For being you," he smiled.

"Davie ! We're going to be late for practice," someone yelled from down the hallway.

Davie laughed. Our fingers were intertwined as he pulled me closer and told me he could stay a little longer.

"Davie, I'm not going on that."

"Katie, yes you are," Davie mocked while nudging my arm.

I smiled at him, and then looked up at the tall roller coaster ahead of us. "Are you serious?"

"Of course, I am. It'll be fun. Besides, I'm here to keep you safe."

I had to laugh at his attempt to sound heroic. "Okay, fine," I agreed.

Davie took my hand and raced to the end of the line. We came to a stop behind a group of guys from school.

I expected Davie to start a conversation with them, so I leaned back against the cool railing.

Davie said "hey" and turned towards me and grasped my waist. He looked into my hazel eyes and whispered, "so are you excited ?"

I smiled. "Yeah, I'm excited, but we have to sit in the front row."

"So, you're not scared anymore?"

"Hah, no. I'm still scared, but you're here to keep me safe," I teased.

Davie laughed and took a step closer to me as he kissed me on my cheek.

"Katie, the grass is so cold !"

"That is why I brought us a lovely blanket."

"Very smart."

"Why thank you, I thought so too," I smiled.

I laid the smooth, blue blanket on the grass and we both sat down. Davie put his arms around my waist and pulled me closer until I was resting against his chest. We watched the sun go down and change from a light pink to violet.

"Skittles ?" Davie asked.

I laughed as he produced an extra-large bag of Skittles from his jacket pocket. We threw away all the colors we didn't like until the grass was scattered with rainbow candies and the palms of our hands were filled with only orange and red.

We popped the Skittles into our mouths and continued watching the sunset. Davie took a strand of my caramel hair and gently put it behind my ear.

I faced him, and he smiled at me. Then he kissed my lips. Cherry was always my favorite flavor.

"Why does the school charge so much for lunch ?" I complained one afternoon.

"Because they can," Davie stated while handing over five dollars to one of the lunch ladies.

"Forget it, I'm just going to get an iced tea. I'll meet you at the table."

"Okay."

I played with my dollar bill until the machine accepted it, then I put in the the random combination of letters and numbers.

I turned around facing the lunch tables and spotted Davie. He was facing the other direction across from Brenda.

I sighed and walked toward the table. Brenda had her eye on Dave since freshman year. She couldn't stand the fact that Davie didn't like her at all, and she hated me for it.

I was standing behind Davie when she looked right at me and said, "why do you even like her?"

My instant reaction was to cut in and tell Davie not to even answer that, but instead he said, "I don't like her." I felt as though someone slapped me in the face.

First, I was shocked, and then completely embarrassed as Brenda began to smirk. I turned away, prepared to run out of the cafeteria all together when Davie said, "I love her, there is a difference."

I spun around feeling entirely stupid and said, "I love you too." Brenda gave me the dirtiest look, but Davie just shifted to face me. "What was that for ?" he blushed.

Chapter 41

Luis

It was Saturday night on July 26, 2008, when I met this boy named Luis. I was downstairs sitting down waiting for my friend to get out of the restroom.

She got out and we were going upstairs to some fifteen party when Luis came up to me and asked me if I had a boyfriend and I said no. He asked me if I could give him my number and I said that I didn't know.

Then he asked for my name, and I told him. We talked for a while. I was shy and nervous; I didn't know what to say.

Finally, I gave him my number. He told me that he was going to call me that night. I said ok, and we both left.

I was surprised because everything happened so fast, and it was weird…

That night I slept over at my sister's house. We got to her house, and we ate.

I told her about the boy I had met. I gave her every detail and told her that I didn't know if I should talk to him because I had just broken up with my ex-boyfriend.

I didn't know if I was ready to talk to someone else. I needed her to give me some advice. She told me to talk to this boy just as friends and to get to know him first and then see what happens.

I told her that I wanted to get over that other one boy I had just broken up. She told me that for me not to worry about that, that I could find someone better and that I was able to talk to whoever I wanted to. That I deserved someone better that treated me good.

She made a positive impact on me because she helped me realize that no boy was worth anything. That right now I shouldn't be worried about no boys, only about school.

But if I really liked someone and I wanted to be with him then I could do it and go ahead and try it.

This really made me feel good and confident about myself. I still didn't know, well I did know if I wanted to talk to him, but I was shy.

He called me almost every day for three weeks. That's how long we talked just to get to know each other better.

Then one day he asked me out when I went to the movies with him. I said yes, I was happy that day.

I really like him, not just because of his looks but because of his personality and other stuff. That's what made me tell him yes. I told my sister, and she was happy for me too.

She told me to make smart choices and to never let no boy put me down again and make me feel like I can't talk to someone else.

Now it's been almost three months since we've been together. Everything is going great, every day I like and care for him more. Hopefully we stay together for some time and be happy just like now.

Chapter 41

The Swing

I was swinging all alone. I could hear it squeak as I went up and down. A cold breeze ran through my bones as a tear rolled down my face.

As usual I had been thinking about you. You said my name. My swing had almost completely stopped. I was shedding tears constantly.

But then I felt something give me a push. Immediately I picked my chin up. I waited until I had stopped moving.

I looked back, and there you were. I said your name leaping from my seat and into your open arms.

I was crying with joy. We hugged. I never wanted to let you go again. If only that moment would have lasted forever, just like our love.

Chapter 42

Summer Love

Lots of people may say that the Seasons of Love is spring, however, I disagree....

The sun burned over the crowd as the wedding was about to begin. The luscious garden was covered with white and red roses that smelled like French vanilla.

A tent covered Central Park where our reception was going to take place. There were beautiful silk fabric drapes everywhere.

I had been looking forward to this day since I proposed to Ada. Standing at the end of the isle, I see my soon-to-be wife as beautiful as I could ever imagine.

Spending the rest of my life with Ada put a smile on my face. I knew she was the one that I was going to be with till I die.

As she walked down the aisle, her maid-of-honor Norma, held her train as the ceremony was about to begin.

Ada and I met two years ago when both of us were backpacking through Italy. Spring in Italy was the most romantic time of the year filled with blooming flowers that were everywhere.

The trees were lush and filled with green leaves. We met at night. There were hundreds of people at the Trevi fountain, but she caught my eye.

I passed by her hoping that she would notice me. I was lucky. She tapped me gently on my shoulder and asked me if I wouldn't mind taking a picture of her and her friend Norma.

I knew I had to say something to her to keep the conversation going so I told her my name.

I asked her where she was from. She told me that she had recently moved to New York from California for work.

I was so surprised to meet a girl that I was interested in all the way in Italy. Her long, dark hair blew in the warm night breeze.

Her blue eyes glistened in the moonlight. I knew I had to have her and see what she was all about.

After that night, we exchanged numbers. We agreed that we should meet for a drink in New York to get to know each other better.

I counted down the days until the day Ada returned to New York where I had been waiting for her.

In my apartment, I walked back and forth trying to get the nerve to call her. I was afraid of rejection.

Maybe she'll think I'm desperate. But then I realized life is about taking chances. I only have one life to live, therefore, I decided to give it a chance and see how it goes.

Drops of sweat started to fall down my face. I dialed her number and the phone started to ring.

Three rings passed and I was just about to give up and hang up the phone. Maybe she didn't want to talk to me. Maybe she is seeing someone. Suddenly a soft voice was heard.

"Hello" the voice whispered

" Hi this is Joe, is this Ada?" I said in embarrassment

"Joe! Yes, its Ada, how are you. How have you been?" She exclaimed.

" I've been good. I just called to see if you wanted to get a bite to eat this week. Maybe Thursday?" I waited anxiously to see what her response would be.

"Of course, I would love to."

I was so excited and shocked that she said yes and after this moment, we were inseparable. We did everything together. From traveling the world to the New York Ranger hockey games. Ada was always by my side.

Two years have passed, and fall has arrived. The beautiful auburn-brown leaves cover the sidewalks and the streets.

The shedding of summer is unavoidable. I can't believe how long ago my wedding day was and how my life has taken a 180 turn like this.

My father always told me that I was too young to get married. I didn't want to listen. What if he was right? Ada and I were so infatuated with each other that we didn't realize how much marriage could change us.

I've been trying to avoid going home. I stay late at work. Seeing Ada's face reminded me of our failed pregnancy attempts. I couldn't help but be angry at her for not getting pregnant.

Sometimes I regret that we got married. A child would have been the only thing to keep this marriage from failing.

I didn't know what to do anymore. The fighting between us had been nonstop this last year. I hated my life, until one day, Norma came from California to visit us.

The three of us ate dinner in town. In the middle of Time Square filled with the hustle and bustle of people everywhere, shimmering multicolored lights lit up the sky.

The fresh, crisp air was refreshing after the last fight with Ada. I felt energized by the New York scene and enjoyed getting lost in the distracting honking of the taxicabs.

We went to the Hard Rock Café. Sitting in a booth in the center of the restaurant, I couldn't help but notice that Ada looked happy. I hadn't seen that in a long time.

I couldn't help but also notice Norma. Her blonde, long silky hair, her beautiful olive-green eyes and her infatuating laugh made me feel intoxicated.

She made me feel like I've known her my entire life. When Norma spoke to me, she would look me straight in the eyes. I felt like the whole room just stopped. Then, she winked at me.

Did Ada just see that? Norma was teasing me, and I needed to get away.

I was confused. I excused myself from the table and walked outside for a few minutes.

Outside of the restaurant I saw a small bar. I just needed to clear my thoughts.

I went into the bar to get a quick drink. Sitting at the bar, I heard her voice behind me,

"Joe?" Norma asked.

"What do you want from me? Why are you here? She is your best friend I don't understand."

" I've never felt like this before Joe. I know she is my best friend, but I need to do what's best for me first.

I am starting to fall for you. From the moment I saw you in Italy, I just knew there was something special about you.

I couldn't say anything because Ada would not stop talking about you. I am not going to hide my feelings anymore and I hope you feel the same way."

She kissed me. I've never felt chemistry like that before. This was the starting point of my two-month affair with Norma.

She moved to New York for me. Being with Norma was easy. I almost forgot what it was like to feel loved and to not fight in a relationship.

She loved me for who I am. For these few months, I lived for the moments that I was able to share with Norma. These few minutes out of the day with her made me feel alive.

I'm going to be a father. Norma told me yesterday that she is pregnant. We are going to start a family together. I'm ecstatic.

Now it's time to end my failed marriage with Ada. I know I must do this. I can't hide this secret from her anymore.

What will she think of me? I can't hurt her any longer, I just need to tell her the truth. It was snowing. It was the gloomiest day of the year.

Chills ran up and down my spine as the cool wind slapped me in the face.

My eyes started to tear from the frosty weather. Walking to our apartment reminded me of all the memories Ada and I had together.

I am about to break her heart and I don't know if this is worth it…

I started to walk up the wet slippery stairs. Every step felt like a stab to my heart.

The beat of my heart echoed in the stairwell. How can I do this to her? Standing outside of the door I could smell my favorite lasagna she made for dinner.

A pool of sweat trickled down my leg and into my damp, cold socks. I unlock the door and enter…

Chapter 43

The Sweetest Aroma

The first thing I noticed as she sat down was her smell. It was so unique and beautiful.

It left an everlasting imprint on my mind. It was as if the freshest flowers all came into bloom at once.

She sat next to me in Math class. She was close enough for me to notice everything about her.

Whether she wore her up or down or a sweatshirt or tee. She was the most beautiful person I have ever laid eyes on.

Everything about her was perfect. Her slightly curly light brown hair. The just brushed the crease on her lower back or her gorgeous deep brown eyes.

Her thin, fit frame from all the hours of working out left her with the body any boy could have wanted but didn't have.

I noticed everything she did like glance at me on the way to class or back track in my direction.

I was hoping that one day that she'll give me a hint. I wanted to know if she liked me as well.

For now, I'll sit near her, intoxicated with her smell, imagining she put it on for me. I started working up the courage to talk to her....

Chapter 44

Love Is a Battlefield

"Ready…. Aim….fire" It was those three little words that the general spoke that crushed soldier Sam's heart.

He was forced to choose between the possible love of his life and the war.

The only reason his family is proud of him is because he is a soldier.

It was love at first sight. When the guns were pointed, and the spears were aimed they knew they were each other's lifelong partner.

Except for there is a few problems. They are on the opposite sides of the war; they are both men and it is absolutely forbidden. These two men will do whatever it takes to be with each other even kill.

"Hey there young man how has your day been?" asked the nurse.

"Well, ya' see I'm in here with a huge gaping hole in my leg and blood everywhere how do you think I am doing?" I responded being pain filled.

"Okay I understand I really do. So other than that, how is it on the battlefield?" the nurse replied with a bit of curiosity in her voice.

"Get this, I was standing there with my rifle pointed directly at the sergeant on the opposing side. Just as General Brad told me to and when he said those three little words, something inside of me wouldn't let me do it.

I tried and tried and tried to get my finger to pull the trigger, but nothing happened.

My finger just wouldn't respond to the message being sent by my brain. I was completely helpless.

The next thing I know is that the General attempts to take my rifle from me and shoot the sergeant himself.

I fight him for it and next thing I know I am on the ground screaming. In massive pain because the damn general shot me on my thigh.

My fellow soldiers took me to the nearest hospital to be aided. Now, I am lying here having a conversation with you" I responded with a bit of snootiness.

"Oh my! What happened to you darling why couldn't you pull that trigger. What was it that was holding' you back sonny?" the nurse questioned me with kindness in her voice.

"Well, my name isn't Sonny it's Tom. To tell you the truth, I don't know what my problem was.

There was a strong force inside of me that told me it wasn't the right thing to do. In that split second when I looked into his eyes, my heart took control of my mind and body and wouldn't let me pull the trigger"

I replied with a hint of shame in my voice. Nurse Brown sat there with a saddened look on her face and wondering what she could do to make Tom feel better.

She sat there and thought for a while. She knew exactly what to do. Suddenly she burst into what she called singing. She began with the song, "where did our love go."

"I've got this burning, burning yearning feeling' inside me Ooh deep inside me and it... hurts... so... bad...?"

I remember laughing hysterically at her wondering what she was doing and why she was doing it.

I paused my hysterical laughter just for a moment and managed to spit out a few words before continuing to laugh.

"WHOA and you call that what?" I questioned her with a bit of interest in my voice.

"Oh… sorry… I was only trying' to make you laugh a little" she replied shyly.

"Well, it worked. You had me scared at first. Then I realized you were doing it out of kindness.

You were only trying to take my mind off the unfortunate situation that took place earlier, thanks" I replied, with a smile that covered my face.

I looked up, whipping the tears from my face. Looking at the nurse, I noticed that she was looking at me as though she was still curious as to why I couldn't truly pull the trigger.

"Tom, if you don't mind me asking what that was truly kept you from pulling that trigger?" she looked on with wonder waiting for a response.

I was hesitant to respond but I did, and I told her the truth.

"Not many people know this about me, but I trust you and I think you're a good person so I will tell you what I think it was.

Now, I'm not like most guys. I don't get all googly eyes when somebody mentions the word breast or sexy women.

I get all tingly inside when someone mentions an attractive young man, with a lean body ripped with muscles.

My heart starts beating fast when I think of a tall dark and handsome man. Anyway, it is true I am gay and there is nothing I can do about it.

I am the way I am so if you don't like it deal with it some other time and patch me up now" he said in a timid voice.

Nurse Brown stood there in surprise, trying to consume all of what she was told. When she finally got everything sorted out, she looked at him with a smile on her face and said, "Hun that isn't anything to be ashamed of, I don't judge people for what they do but by who they are and how they act.

I think you should be allowed to express yourself just as you please. Now tell me what it about him is that caught your' eye?" Nurse Brown replied with a smile on her face.

Soldier Tom sat there looking at Nurse Brown with that look of curiosity as to why she was so accepting of him. When he finally replied he said this, "Well it was like I knew he was meant for me.

I had this deep feeling inside me telling me that whoever made him knew that I would need someone to live my life with, and that is why he was created just for me...."

Right in the middle of his sentence the sergeant was being brought in on a stretcher with a bullet wound to his knee.

The wound looked like it hurt, but the way the sergeant was acting told us a whole different story.

The sergeant lay there singing along to the ever so popular song Wild Thing by the Troggs.

He sat up in the middle of his singing to see what everyone was laughing at. "What is so funny if I may ask?" he asked with a snooty voice

"Nothing just thought it was a little funny that you are singing when you look as though you are in such pain. I have never met anyone else who does that." Tom replied with excitement.

"Wow I felt the exact same way. All my fellow soldiers seem to think I am strange and most of them don't except me for who I am." He said with a sigh.

"Just because you sing when in pain?" I asked curiously

"Well, that and ah some other reasons" he said with shame.

"What is it if I may ask?" I asked him with kindness surrounding my question.

"Well, I am uhhh gay" he responded with a shy voice as though I would be disgusted.

"If you are just trying to yank my chain don't do it, because when I saw you on the battlefield I was absolutely love struck.

I couldn't shoot you so the general shot me, and that's why I'm in here and I was hoping to see you soon.

I wanted to tell you just how I felt." After I confessed my feelings to the sergeant, I sat there with a look on my face saying to myself to please love me back.

The war soon ended, and we planned on going our separate ways, but faith had another idea.

While I was boarding my bus to leave, I heard the sergeant screaming my name. I turned to see him running full speed to me with a smile covering his face.

He convinced me to come home with him and meet his family. I accepted the gesture.

During the long trip back home, we had a lot of time to connect with each other and learn more.

We decided that we would live out our lives together remembering that faith filled day and never forgetting that love is a battlefield.

Chapter 45

Winters Trap

Along a path we walked seemed like forever…

I stared romantically at my boyfriend wondering if my parents would ever find me. We were headed towards the mountains.

He says there is a cottage he built with his father a long time ago. No one knows where it is but him.

I think back to when we agreed to run away from our parents. It was the only reason we would ever become close.

Our parents put us in a class because they thought we were crazy for the rebelling phrase we went through.

I said I was going to burn the government and demand changes around the world.

He had the same idea, except, not so gruesome. He wanted to make a banner symbolizing what we are.

What is to come and put it every well-known place to spread the word, eventually having a group of people following in his footsteps.

Eventually, everything was taking force. They noticed what we were doing.

His ideas were amazing, I really thought it would work, if his mother didn't find the blueprints to every popular site around the world.

The fact his Journal looked like he wanted to rule the world with his justice.

"How much longer?" I asked him while holding his hand on the stick shift of the car.

"Not too much longer until we hit the mountain. Were basically on it." When we got to the little cottage, I was telling you about it.

We can start planning what we're going to do from there. You know our families will look for us for a while and eventually give up.

When we stay up there, no one will know that were in the mountains. There is no trace of us going here, no journal, no plans; because it was a verbal talk during the private session we had together.

Everything will be lovely, just you and me, on the mountain, with lots of snow, and maybe kids. Its paradise."

"I sure do love the snow. Kids will be fine after we get married." The car started to rattle and broke down. "Babe what's wrong with the car?" I was concerned to what was going on. "I'll go check, you stay here and be as warm as you can."

He jumped outside and checked all around the car. I looked out into the horizon only to see untouched snow and the sunset making the snow brighter than it appears.

It's so beautiful, I will love living up here for the next 2 months. "Babe?"

"Yeah?" I replied, he opened the door and stared at me.

"We must walk the rest of way; the truck is stuck in the snow. Come on let's go."

Just my luck, I thought to myself.

I just shook my head as we walked towards the sun. We held hands as it became dark and very cold.

The winds were harsh and started to develop into a harsh blizzard, I held on to him has we kept walking into what seemed like to our death.

A cold winter's night with the rushed snow blowing in my ear. We walked that seemed like forever.

"I can't walk anymore Willie." I complained as I tried to lift my leg from the 4 foot snow.

"Come on babe, the cave is right ahead. I'm right here with you. I won't leave you I promise."

His smile had a warm feeling that made me smile a little bit. But I still think we're going to die.

I looked ahead and saw the black sky in front of me, and the white harsh snow rushing in front of my eyes.

Suddenly I saw it, the cave he was talking about. We walked in the cave when the ground started to shake.

I tried catching my balance, but I fell upon his chest listening to his heart. I looked up at him and he just smiled.

The shaking of the ground stopped; I looked around. The entrance was blocked, no way out. Now I know where going to die.

"We're trapped" I pointed out worriedly.

"At least were together"

"We have nothing but our clothes. Our food supplies are in the cabin where we're supposed to be."

"Have faith, okay? Everything will be fine"

"Faith? In what?"

"The light will show us the way," he said while sitting down at the edge of the cave.

"Do you want to die?" I was still standing below him.

"I mean, we're going to be rescued I can feel it. Just have faith that they will find us and dig us out."

"Of our grave" I said folding my arms and eventually rubbing them. I had a snow outfit, but it's never enough after a while."

He smiled at me and stood up, beginning to wrap his arm around my waist and kissed me.

He held me tight and released his lips upon mine. "I read that if people cuddle, there body warm will warm both of the bodies."

I smiled because I knew he just wanted love, and to make me feel better. I cuddled into his chest. He always knew best.

"Well, I'm tired, I am going to sleep. Don't let go of me. Or I will die. It will be all your fault." He kiddingly said.

I punched him in the arm. "That's not nice." I paused and watched him lying down on the ground. "Wow its cold."

"Then come over here and cuddle with me. We'll both be warm." He smiled up at me while I lay on his chest.

"You know your right. When we wake up, we'll be saved, and in Hawaii, where it's warm." I fell asleep listening to his heartbeat.

Hours passed when I awoke listening to nothing. I stood up and started shaking Willie. He wouldn't wake up.

I grasp hold of him crying my eyes out. Suddenly the dark cave began to lighten up. There they were the Rescue team here to rescue us.

Too bad it was too late for him. They tried to get me away from the body, but I couldn't let go.

I loved him so much. I didn't tell him that. But eventually, they got me away from the body and took him away, while trying to warm me up.

They checked the body and found that around his heart was hypothermia the reason why he died. His hands and feet were black, like his chest was.

He never told me he couldn't feel anything because he loved me.

Chapter 46

Just You and I

Over the summer I met the most amazing girl named Cathy at the beach. She had beautiful flowing blonde hair and sparkling blue eyes.

I'm not going to lie, but she was hot! It was love at first sight. I introduced myself to her and she couldn't stop smiling.

I knew that she was into me by how shy she was when she talked. I was so nervous to get to know her because I was just a skinny boy with no muscle or tan or anything.

I didn't know what kind of person she was attracted to, but I tried to have confidence.

She was so cute I couldn't get over it. I finally asked her out to dinner on Friday night and she accepted. She took my phone out of my hand and put her number in it and said, "call me". My stomach dropped.

That was only the beginning. After Cathy and I had been together for almost ten months, we were deeply in love.

One day after school, everything changed. I had always told her that I would be loyal, but she never believed me.

She hadn't talked to me in days, and I didn't know why. She had left me these mean voicemails on my phone about how all guys are the same. She knew that I wouldn't be able to be tied down to one girl.

She was so mad over something that I had no idea about. She told me that she has clear evidence that I had been cheating with another girl.

She told me that over the passed few days I had been acting weird and distant.

She felt like things just weren't the same. I didn't know what she meant. "I had my reasons for being distant" I had told her, "But I didn't cheat".

She claims that there was a long brown hair lying on his computer, which couldn't have been hers because she had light blonde hair, and he didn't have a sister who could have been the owner either.

She also saw the flower store website up on my computer screen and knew that those couldn't be for her because there wasn't any holiday or anniversary coming up that they could be for her.

She wouldn't return my phone calls or texts or anything. I thought she was going to leave me for good and never wanted to talk to me again.

I couldn't handle that. I loved her so much. I had done nothing wrong. Secretly, I had been out shopping for days to try to buy her a promise ring. The flowers just because I loved her.

I wanted to surprise her. I had gone out with her sister to try to find the right one. She wouldn't even talk to me. I couldn't tell her the truth without ruining the surprise. I didn't know what to do.

I had an idea so that I might still surprise her. I called her mom while she was at work and told her the truth and the whole story behind why Cathy. I also told why we haven't been talking.

I arranged for me to go in their house and surprise her in my own way. I went in while everyone was at work and put a path of white rose petals all the way upstairs to her room.

I lit candles all around her room and put a dozen red roses and the ring in the box on her bed.

I hid in her closet waiting for her to come home. I heard the door open and her franticly walk up the stairs.

I knew she had to be confused. She shot into her room and went over to the bed and started to tear up.

I popped out of the closet and wrapped my arms around her. I explained to her that that hair she found was her sister's because I took her with me to pick out her ring.

The flower website was for her. It was all for her. I was loyal and I didn't lie. It was all for the better of our relationship.

We finally were able to trust each other, and she started to not be so bothered by anything I was doing.

She used to completely blow up my phone every time I was out anywhere just to make sure I wasn't cheating on her or doing something that she wouldn't like. We finally passed that, and everything was good.

The following week, I was at home working on my homework to keep my grades up so that I could get into a good college.

That is what my parents so desperately wanted. I needed to start being more efficient. Cathy knew I needed time to study and had a hair appointment at Glitz salon, just down the street from her house. She'll tell you the story from here.

I pulled up to the salon and I was five minutes early for my appointment, which excited me because I could have a sit down and read a magazine, which was one of my favorite parts.

I picked up the Glamour magazine from the top of the coffee table and opened it up to the middle. It was an ad for lip gloss of course.

Right then, I felt a soft breeze hit my face. I shivered a little, and a guy sat beside me. It was Jose, my ex-boyfriend and first love.

"Hi Cathy! "He was a tall muscular guy with a nice tan and a gorgeous smile!

"Oh, hi Jose! How have you been?"

"I've been good how about you?"

"Great," We kept up with the small talk until my hairdresser called me back to the chair to get my hair done.

"Well, it's time for me to go back," I said.

"Oh, that's okay, maybe after our appointments we can get together for some lunch to catch up".

"Sounds good to me, I'll meet ya at the café down the street in an hour". I walked back to the chair and sat down.

All I could think of was Jose and our past. How much fun we used to have, and how much I missed him every day.

Then Jake popped into my head. "How would Jake feel about this?" I knew that he trusted me, and I could get away with it without him even finding out that we went out to lunch. It wasn't a big deal.

Sitting there getting my hair cut and blow dried I had racing thoughts. Thoughts about what might happen, or where this lunch could go.

I wanted to make sure Jake never found out about this. I love him, but I love Jose too.

I admit I still have some feelings for Josh, even though I convinced myself that I didn't.

We had only broken up because his mom had died, and he was too emotionally unstable to have a girlfriend.

He seemed to be doing okay now. I wondered if this was some kind of sign, how he had popped back into my life. I took off my ring that Jake had given me and slipped it into my pocket.

After I left the salon, I quickly walked down the road into town where the café was.

I didn't know if Jose was already there or not, but I sure didn't want to wait outside and risk the chance of someone seeing me and telling Jake.

I went inside. Jose had already been seated in a little booth towards the back of the restaurant waiting for me.

I sat down and right away we started talking like we hadn't even been apart. It was weird.

Jake and I had never talked like this. This was the best date I've ever been on. I felt so happy to finally see him again and catch up.

He was the perfect guy. But I did feel bad about going behind Jake's back.

After lunch I had to go back home and start working on homework of my own. It was awkward trying to say goodbye because neither of us wanted to.

I felt these butterflies in my stomach that I used to get when he looked at me. He leaned in for what I thought was going to be an innocent hug and he kissed me.

I felt my stomach drop and I kissed back. He grabbed me and held me close. He told me that he missed me and wished we could be back together again. I started to tear up again.

Then suddenly, I felt my phone in my pocket vibrate, it was Jose. I ignored it and slid it back in my pocket.

Back at home, Jose was concerned. "Why wouldn't she answer my calls?" I thought to myself. "She had to be out of the salon by now..."

I was starting to get worried because I was blowing up her phone and she still hadn't answered.

Maybe I should go try to check up on her. I hoped that everything was okay. I walked down the road to the salon that she always went to and went inside.

The lady at the fount desk said that she had left over an hour ago and said she was going to the café down the road for lunch.

So, I left. I headed the other way down the road again and I saw her there on the sidewalk outside of the café.

I walked closer because I saw that she wasn't alone. She was kissing someone! I thought, "This couldn't be Cathy, it must be someone else," I got closer and sure enough it was.

She is cheating on me. She went behind my back and hooked up with another guy!

So many thoughts and emotions were running through my head I didn't know what to say or what to do.

I could feel my whole body heating up and the sweat trickled down my neck.

Between breaths she looked up and saw me standing there. She turned away pretending to be someone else.

"How could you do this to me!" I turned and started to walk away, tears filling my eyes.

"It's not what it looks like, I'm sorry!" She ran after me.

"How could you do this to me? After all we've been through, after I bought you that ring! It was all a lie, you never loved me. You are so fake!"

I burst into tears and started to walk away. I took off the necklace that she bought me from Florida and threw it at her feet.

As it bounced off the sidewalk into the street and turned the other way. Right then I knew it was over. She was my life and now she was gone. My world was gone.

After months had passed full of sorrow and pain, I began to get over her. I started to move on and hang out with new people, new girls.

There wasn't any that I met that would ever match up to Cathy, but eventually I knew that special girl would come along and make me completely forget about Cathy.

Until then, I decided that there were more important things in life and that I had to live it up while I still had time.

My life wasn't over, I just came upon a rough patch and things finally were starting to smooth over. It wasn't the end of the world after all.

Chapter 47

The First Kiss

I stroked my fingers through her hair. The tension between us is rising. She and I both know it's coming.

I lean my head towards her, and she does the same. Our lips connect like magnets.

The perfect kiss. After about 8 sec I slowly pulled my face away from her face and put it so that my nose would relate to her nose.

She looks at me eagerly and smiles. We stayed in that position for about 5 minutes.

Just by that kiss, we know more about each other than we could ever know. We were saving it for when we knew we were truly right for each other.

Now, we are certain that there's nothing that can break this bond between true love.

Chapter 48

Dreams Change Lives

As he passed by me, my head started spinning and the shadow that was in my dream last night popped right into my head.

It can't be said to myself. His face is identical to the one in my dream, but I don't know him.

I can't know him. I'm new to this school. There is no possible way that I've ever seen him in my life but as I investigated his face. It felt like I should have known that face. It is like I've been seeing it all my life.

As soon as the bell rang, I walked right out of my seat and went to my second period class.

The rest of the day went by quickly. As I walked home with my friend Bella, I told her about the dream I had and how that guy I saw earlier in the day looked exactly like the one in my dream.

I had never seen him in my life before except today. She said that it was possibly a coincidence and not to worry about it.

That didn't help. All through the rest of the day the image I saw in my dream came right into my head.

The truth was I didn't get to see the guy in my dream very clearly because as I said before, it was like a shadow but still the image that I got to see in my dream, was like the guy at school today.

I couldn't sleep very well although the night. I still managed to fall asleep. The dream I had today made it clear.

The guy I had seen at school today was the guy in my dream. In this dream I was about to turn around to talk to him but then I woke up.

I was so mad. I wanted to scream but I decided not to wake my parents up. I took a shower instead....

Chapter 49

Class Reunion

It had almost been a decade since I've even given that a thought. I started wondering if I should go……

My friends and I had pledged that we would try and make it to any school gathering each year, but well, I gave up on that thought the very year I graduated.

As I held the invitation, this time, something within me urged me to participate in it.

What the heck, I could use another night out, I told myself.

I started calling a few of my old school buddies and convinced them to make it there. They were quite surprised to hear the all-new vigor in me to go to the reunion this year.

Let me inform you that there was a lot of anticipation of that reunion. The D-day arrived and on that warm evening.

I expected nothing extraordinary, just a few plump men, and a gang of chattering women.

I must confess that inside I felt excitement that I hadn't felt for a long time.

Being in the entertainment industry, parties were what I indulged in, for a living. But then, something was different this time, or was it just my lousy intuition?

The reunion at the Hilton hotel was nice, quite interesting. As the party set in, it was great!

It was fun seeing my old friends with nicknames like "curly" now with great big bald patches.

We laughed and talked like little kids in their ninth grade. It was fun, and I wondered why I had never bothered with reunion parties all these years.

I walked up to the bar counter to get myself another drink. I excused myself through groups of middle-aged teenagers in their twenties and thirties, spilling beer as they laughed.

The reunion was fun, I reminded myself. With a drink in my hand, I walked back across the room.

I was lost in my thoughts as I unknowingly elbowed someone in a bunch of giggling women. I pulled myself together and apologized to her. She was very pretty and accepted the apology gracefully. Her eyes were charming.

I walked passed, and her eyes reminded me of a beautiful memory. Something I couldn't have lost but had tried to forget during all these years.

My heart missed a beat and began to pound hard. Could it be her? I turned around and wished for a miracle.

Oh my god, it is Maria!

This was the very same girl who stole my dreams each night many years ago. I could tell it was her with just a glance. I could never forget those lovely eyes. She was beautiful and hadn't changed a bit since I last saw her.

I stumbled to a chair as I tried to hold my heart within my chest. I was panicking. I felt like a little boy we read about in those love stories. The same way I always felt when she was around.

Memories of my teenage love began to pop in my head…

The first time I felt this way, I was in ninth grade. I was one of those kids you call a dorky middle bencher, not too geeky, but not cool enough to fit in, at the back of the class I always sat.

There was this new girl in school. The teacher introduced her to the class. Her name was Maria. I wanted to be her friend, but each time I walked up to her, I just froze and ended up with a guilty grin.

One day in class, I whispered to the girl sitting next to me to introduce me to Maria. She just smiled and kept quiet. When the bell rang and the teacher walked out, this girl just stood up and shouted out at the top of her voice, much to my confusion, "Maria, this guy, John likes you!!"

The class burst out laughing and yes, Maria laughed out too. I just wanted to hide under the bench. I felt so stupid.

For the rest of the term, I just sat very quietly and contemplated. Finally, I told Maria that I liked her. She told me that we can go out that evening. It was all unplanned. As always, I made a big mess of everything. She put me out of my misery with a well-placed 'No'. That no was the answer to what I asked. I asked her to be my girl. My heart was shattered into pieces.

I couldn't speak much to her after that day. I was too scared. I would tell her that I liked her, occasionally, which made me look more stupid. I used to call her, every now and then. It felt good listening to her voice.

All the calls ended when her dad installed a caller id which was relatively new back then. She got to know it was me who used to call her at all hours of the night. Maria got very angry.

She called me up the next day. She told me that I was a 'psycho' and tried telling me that there were better things to talk about than just "can I meet you after school?"

She was the one who taught me the sentence "how's the weather?", and told me to ask her that, each time I wanted her out.

Two years had passed and there wasn't much I could do to get over this girl. I even brought her cards that I never gave her. I recorded cassettes that I couldn't give her, though I used to neatly write her name on each tape.

Graduation day passed by, and we parted ways with interesting pet names for each other. She called me a "psycho", and well, I called her "princess" though I could never say that out loud.

I tried forgetting her, but it was something I couldn't do. I dated a few girls and got my life back in place. I lost the middle bencher tag, and got the new tag, "charming". Wish I could have had the same tag back in school. But well, I learned a new line all by myself though. "Shit happens".

As I was walking to my table, I had a blast from the past…

A smack on my shoulder had me back in my senses, along with a splash of vodka on my thigh. It was one of the guys staring at me. The guys got around me and wondered if I was too drunk.

I was, I really was, and only I knew it wasn't just the drink. In my mind, I was in the middle of a teenage boy's love story.

I pointed out across the room, and they followed my finger. The guys were stunned too, only for a second, until they burst out laughing.

A few hands grabbed my shirt, and a few let their hands fall hard on my sorry back. They couldn't believe that someone could make me get weak in the knees even after so long. I couldn't believe it either!

I never was the one who had any trouble approaching or picking up girls, but right now, I felt like the teenage boy who was in love with a girl in class.

I knew I could never walk up to her and start talking. She would still assume that I was a psycho. I really wanted to make a fast and good impression with her. I was pretty sure she wouldn't recognize me now. I had lost my thick glasses, and my loser attitude.

My friends motivated me to approach her. They didn't know I was still scared to talk to this girl. I just shrugged them and pretended like I didn't care about her.

I had to let her know I was smooth before I approached her. I knew just what to do. This was impression time, and this was my only chance.

I walked up to one of my old teachers. After a brief conversation, I had a good old microphone in my hands in just a few minutes.

I wasn't a good MC for nothing. I have proven that I was among the best in all the parties, but right now, I feel like this was my biggest and most hard-to-please audience.

I called out to the crowd, and I felt my confidence ooze back into me, my voice through the speakers always had that effect on me! I had the audience laughing and indulging in games and crazy activities.

I tried hard not to stare at Maria. I could see her from the corner of my eye. She whispers to her friends occasionally.

Now that's a good sign! She recognized me… wow! This is going to be fun. I wondered what she might be thinking. "Can this really be him, the same psycho from school?"

I walked off the stage with roaring applause, and a Superhuman ego! I loved what I just did.

I walked pass Maria and pretended like I didn't see her. Man, I wanted to talk to her so bad! But I knew what I had to do, and I wasn't going to screw it up. I had to play my cards right.

Later, that evening, we had one of those group games that are played in school reunions.

It was just the moment I had been waiting for, the Team Building game, where people had to form groups in certain numbers or be eliminated.

I made sure I would be in the same group as Maria. It will be in one of the rounds. For the first time that night, I braved eye contact. I looked at her, with a bit of surprise, and just stared. Fake recognition dawned upon me! It was Maria.

"Maria?" I blurted out in fake astonishment. I had to use a lot of fake emotions that night.

She smiled. Oh god, my heart gave an instant meltdown. Our group was eliminated from the game, because of the wrong number of people. But who cares, I knew I won.

I could see it in her eyes. It wasn't the same "I see a psycho" look from the school days. It was warm, and more than friendly.

I pulled a chair back for her to sit down. She smiled. Courage rules! We sat down and spoke. I spoke like I had never spoken to her. We laughed and talked the entire night.

She told me about how pleasantly surprised she was to see this new person in me. I told her how nice it was to see her after all these years. I still feel the same way I did in school. She admired it. I could have melted right there.

I asked her out to dinner, and both of us took off to one of the quiet restaurants in the hotel.

We talked and talked, and I could see the warmth in her beautiful eyes that felt so good. We spoke about all the stupid things I did back then and laughed it off together.

We took a walk by the garden and sat down on one of the garden benches. I held her hand and told her how happy I was to see her again.

She smiled as she placed her other hand on mine. "Same here, John… same here."

Chapter 50

A Summer Romance

It was a warm summer afternoon. There was just a glimpse of the sun above the horizon. I felt a slight breeze, brushing lightly against my skin. I could feel my dark brown hair flowing with the direction of the wind as I went around and around on the carousel.

I closed my eyes and listened to the carnival music. In the background, I could also hear people talking and laughing.

Even with my eyes closed, I could still see the joyful faces of the children. Their eyes are wide open with excitement, their parents watching them carefully and happily. I smiled, capturing the moment.

I made sure to mentally write down all the details in my head, so I could retell it exactly to my parents.

It's been nearly a week since I last seen them and would be another month or two until I see them again, although before leaving they made me promise to call them whenever I wanted but at least, once a week.

Their 20th anniversary was last week, so as my gift, I decided to go stay with my aunt in California for the summer.

As my mind wandered to my home back in New York, I felt the carousel slowly come to a stop. I gently opened my eyes and let out a happy sigh. I laughed as I struggled to get off my carousel horse. Feeling dizzy, I went to find a place to sit.

As I sat down on a nearby bench, my eyes swept the carnival for a hot dog stand. Aha. Seeing one, I started walking towards it. Halfway there, knowing I was supposed to call my aunt at 9:30.

I decided to see what time it was. I looked down in my bag and began searching for my phone. Suddenly, I ran into someone. "Sorry-", I looked up unexpectedly into the striking blue eyes of a drop-dead gorgeous stranger. He looked about my age, if not a year older. He was an inch taller than me. No words could even begin to describe him.

My heart pounding, I tried to catch my breath. Just when I thought he couldn't get any hotter, Gorgeous Stranger smiled, making his eyes twinkle and my conclusion rip into shreds…

Finally, catching my breath again, I tried to speak again. "Sorry, I wasn't watching where I was going.

He laughed, and then smiled again. "Don't be", he said. Even the sound of his voice made my heart explode. He held out his hand. "I'm Robert, by the way "I held out my hand, meeting his. My hand tingled. "Dolores" I said back, matching his smile.

"Do you live around here? I don't think I've seen you around town before." Deep breaths, deep breaths, I thought to myself. "N-No, I'm just visiting my aunt for the summer.

I live in New York. What about you??" I asked. "I moved here about five years ago from New Jersey, so I've lived here for some time.

"How long are you staying with your aunt?" His eyes seemed to sink into mine; making it appear each thing I said really mattered.

As if I really mattered. My heart fluttered as though it were a butterfly trying to escape.

The odd, yet amazing thing was, that, even though it was breathe taking. I loved the feeling of excitement.

I wanted to jump up and scream, as though a bubbly volcano had erupted. I could feel it building inside me, as his eyes continued to stare into mine.

I loved the way hero, wait, he asked me a question. It was hard to concentrate on anything when I was staring at him. He was so gorgeous.

I was doing it again. Okay, Okay, answer the question. "F-F-For the summer", I said. Hahn! Why do I keep stuttering? He probably thinks I have a speaking disorder, I thought. He smiled again."

"Cool, maybe we can hang out sometime. I could show you around town, if you like", he said. Oh yes, I would like, Very Much…. "Sure, that sounds like fun."

When would, I started to ask, but suddenly I was cut off. "Robert! I've been looking all over for you."

I turned to see who rudely interrupted me and saw a beautiful blonde walking toward us with two almost as equally gorgeous girls, one taller, the other average height. The one who was taller was also blonde, but the average height one was a brunette.

Judging by the way the beautiful blonde was walking just slightly ahead of them, I could tell she was the leader of their group.

Also, judging by the look she was giving me, I could tell she wasn't too fond of me. Great, I already have someone who hates my guts. I sighed. Super. They all seemed to walk in unity, and as if they owned the place, like they were better than everyone else.

Their eyes weren't exactly friendly. As they got closer, I could see two guys with them, who seemed to trail the other two like puppies, obviously their boyfriends.

I realized in disappointment that the leader didn't seem to have one, but apparently wanted one, by the seducing look she was giving Robert.

My stomach turned. "Hey Gloria. Hey Sam, hey Jenny. What's up Willie?" Robert said to them all, giving me an apologetic look.

So, the leader was Gloria, the two behind her were Sam and Jenny, and the guys were Willie and Carlos, I thought, hoping I could remember which is which.

As they reached where we were standing, Gloria went and stood by Robert; very close, I might add, while the others sort of circled around.

Gloria wrapped her arms around Robert. "Where have you been, we looked all over for you!" she said. She gave me a dirty look. "Who are you? Someone called 911?

I smiled at my little sarcastic comment and was tempted to laugh when I saw that my little grin seemed to annoy Gloria. Robert, however, seemed to look amused again.

With a deep breath, I told myself that I would remain neutral if anything should happen. At least for now, He He. "Hi, I'm Dolores. I'm visiting here from New York for the summer. "Nice." I smiled to myself. Let's just hope I can stay calm for the rest of the night.

Chapter 51

The License

One beautiful spring day in 1954, Paul and Anne headed to a courthouse for a license. Anne never questioned Paul because they were always up to something. They love making plans and enjoy each other company.

On that day, Paul told Anne that it would be nice to go to the lake and do some fishing. Anne reminded him that a fishing permit was required. If they were going soft water fishing, it was necessary to have a fishing license. At the beach, no license was needed.

So, they got into their car and headed to the courthouse....

As they walked in the building, Paul began to smile. Anne thought that he was acting kind of weird. She has known him since they were in grammar school. They were neighbors, therefore, both families knew that someday they would fall in love.

Paul asked the clerk about the different licenses issued by the court and the cost for each one. The clerk explained to him that a fishing license cost $1.50, gun permit, which cost at that time, $3.00 and a marriage license cost $2.50.

Anne was kind of puzzled with all the questions Paul kept asking about licenses. They both were there for a fishing license. She didn't care about any other license.

Paul and Anne were 21 years old, high school graduates and both had jobs. Money was no problem for either one of them.

Without even asking Anne, Paul just smiled d and asked the clerk to give him the forms for a marriage license.

They had a beautiful wedding. All their friends and family members were at church and later at the reception.

They bought a big house which was later filled with four children.

Whenever they had a disagreement, Anne would remind Paul that he could have saved money if he had chosen a fishing license. Anne also told him that the fishing license would expire in a year.

The extra dollar cost Paul 60 years of a happy marriage with the girl of his dreams.

Chapter 52

A Beautiful Romance

He left a single red rose on my windshield. He wasn't allowed to send me flowers at work, since my husband had died only six months ago.

When the time was right, he sent me flowers on my birthday, Valentine's Day, and eventually every anniversary.

The guys at work told him he made them look bad. They were joking, but he wasn't.

He kept sending me flowers. He made me breakfast in bed. Most importantly, he invited my daughter and her three children to move in with us after she split from her then-husband. What's more romantic than that?

Chapter 53

Reunited in New York City

The moment Matilda met David aboard the ship, she knew he was someone special. He became her first love. They had a situation and that was that they live 2,000 miles apart…

After the cruise, we maintained our love affair through text messages and phone calls. We were happy for the first couple of weeks; however, things began to happen. I feel as if something was missing from this long-distance relationship.

Eventually, geography took its toll. We went on to separate lives. I thought about him quite often.

Thirty years later, we reunited in New York. He hired a violinist to play our love song. We held each other for the first time in three decades.

After talking for long hours about their thirty years separation, they made plans.

Chapter 54

The Bicycle Ride

It is the year 1975, when Charlotte, a 19-year-old student of a Swedish royal family, travels to India to get a portrait made by a gifted artist.

The artist was born into a poor Indian family of the lowest caste, also known as the "untouchables."

Despite the incredibly difficult circumstances, the artist named Pradyumna Kumar Mahanandia had gained an outstanding reputation for being a gifted painter.

His reputation led Charlotte Von to travel all the way to India to get her portrait done.

By the time the portrait was finished, the two had fallen in love. Pradyumna was fascinated with Charlotte's beauty.

Never had he seen a more beautiful woman from the Western world. He did his best to capture all her beauty in the portrait, yet never fully succeeded.

Nonetheless, the portrait was magnificent, and Charlotte fell for his simplicity and his beautiful character.

Because of him, she spontaneously decided to stay longer in India. Out of a couple of days became weeks and then even months. The two had fallen so deeply in love that they decided to get married according to traditional Indian rituals.

Unfortunately, the time came when Charlotte had to leave again to complete her studies in London.

Thousands of miles separated the two but their feelings for each other never changed.

They stayed in contact through letters, which they exchanged almost weekly with each other.

Naturally, the newlyweds struggled terribly with the great distance between each other. Charlotte offered her husband to buy him air tickets, which he refused.

He had not only decided to complete his studies first, but he had also set his mind on reuniting with the love of his life on his own terms. He even made her the promise that he would do anything he could to see her again.

After Pradyumna had finished his studies, he took all his possessions and sold them.

Unfortunately, the money he earned didn't even come close to a flight ticket. All he could afford was a cheap and used bicycle.

Many would have been greatly disappointed; some would have even given up. But not Pradyumna.

Instead of allowing the difficult circumstances to stop him from seeing his beloved wife again, he made the decision to use what he had to see her again.

Nothing could stop him from reuniting with his wife, even if that meant an exhausting bicycle ride half around the world.

His decision was the beginning of a bicycle journey from India to the Western world.

Pradyumna took all his paintings and brushes along with him to financially support his endeavor.

His voyage led him through eight countries and took more than four months. But eventually, he arrived at Charlotte's hometown in Sweden and finally saw her again. From then on, the two never left each other's side for too long.

Chapter 55

The Mountain Man

There are people who say love can move mountains. This might not be physically possible, but Joaquin, also known as the "Mountain man", came close.

Joaquin and Dora have been married for over forty years. They had five children that left their home to live in the big cities.

So, Joaquin and Dora had no one to look after them. They didn't want to leave their cottage which was located up in the mountains on a small island.

One day, Joaquin's wife Dora, fell while crossing a nearby hill. She hurt herself very seriously. She needed quick medical assistance, however, that wasn't possible due to the hill that isolated their small village from the next town.

Unfortunately, his wife died from the serious injuries before Joaquin could do anything about it.

It was the same night when Joaquin decided to carve a small path through the mountain to give his village easier access to the hospital.

Joaquin was determined to achieve his plan. He was heavily teased for it. But after working for over twenty years with the greatest determination and willpower, a path was carved into the hill.

Even though he was initially ridiculed and mocked for his mission to give his hometown easier access to the nearby town, he finally succeeded.

His life's work helped to reduce the distance between the two towns from 65 km to only 15 km.

Never again the Mountain man and his neighbors suffered pain or any real tragedy because the mountains are now connected with nearby towns.

Chapter 56

A Special Prom Night

Albert and his mother always had a unique bond with each other. You see, Albert's father died at war.

Albert never met him. His mother, Nelly, took care of him all by herself. She didn't remarry, even though she was very pretty and talented. Albert was her world. He would spend hours with her.

Albert was always ready to listen to his mother's stories of a lifetime. She once told him that she had met his father long time after graduating from high school.

Let me also tell you that Nelly went to an all-girl school. This was also the reason why she was never asked out to go to the prom.

When the day of Albert's prom had arrived, his mother was so excited for him. She had watched him save money for months so that he could afford a tuxedo and even a limousine.

His mother enthusiastically waited to find out who Albert would be taking to the prom.

But to her great surprise, he told her that he would be taking her to the prom. He told her that every woman deserves to go to a prom, no matter if they are 18 or 40.

Mother and son had the greatest time ever on that special prom night.

Chapter 57

The Promise

When Victoria saw Mario, an Italian tennis player, during a contest on TV, she immediately became interested in him. She was so determined to meet the athlete that she kept asking the TV commentators for his phone number, email, etc.

Victoria never gave up. She bothered everyone on the TV until they finally gave in.

Once she had his email address, she contacted him, and they both agreed to meet. It was love at first sight and the two married not long after meeting for the first time.

The young tennis player moved for his wife to the United States. He applied for the U. S. citizenship. He was so in love with her that he also promised her that he would one day bring her an Olympic medal.

Mario was determined to live up to his promise, but things came differently....

In 2017, his beautiful wife Victoria died in a car accident. It was an unimaginable tragedy for the young man.

Mario never forgot the promise he had made Victoria. He remembered what he had promised his beautiful wife.

It was the promise that kept him going through this difficult time. He became so determined that he was finally selected to become part of the United States Olympic team at the 2018 Olympics.

During the competition, Mario was faced with incredibly challenging competitors. He had three match attempts but failed in two.

Seeing his chances of ever reaching the platform diminishing. He put everything he had left into the third and final attempt.

As luck would have it, he managed to play two games, which won him the Olympic gold medal.

The part when he was awarded the medal was broadcast to millions of viewers all around the world. Mario simply couldn't help himself. He broke out into tears while holding a picture of his wife Victoria into the cameras.

Chapter 58

Just Pure Love

In 2011, bomb disposal expert James Adams was severely injured after the explosion of an improvised bomb in Afghanistan.

The explosion took all his limbs. It really changed the life of the 20-year-old United States soldier forever.

While recovering from the injuries in a military hospital, Adams was confronted with the painful realization that his limbs had gone.

He also had to face the fact that he would be dependent on assistance for the rest of his life.

It was an incredibly difficult situation not only for him, but also his family and especially his longtime girlfriend Linda.

Instead of ever giving him up, Linda became James' support in life. She helped him recover and took care of him during this incredibly challenging time.

Linda played an important role in James' quick recovery. She never went away from his side and assisted him greatly.

When he learned to walk again with his new prosthetic limbs, she was there for him.

After James had recovered, he proposed to his beloved girlfriend, and they got married.

This is really a beautiful ending of an incredibly inspiring love story that shows that nothing can ever stand in-between two people who really love each other.

Chapter 59

The Happy Ending

Ray and Anne were the life of the party. Ever since they got married, right after college, they moved into the biggest house in upstate New York. Their friends were all upper class.

Both Ray and Anne were hard workers. Both had a law degree. Anne adored her husband. Ray couldn't face any new adventure without Anne. They were meant for each other since grammar school.

One summer evening, the young couple were invited to a cookout way up in the mountains.

Ray knew his way up the Catskills, but as they were heading for the party, it began to rain. It got very dark too soon. Ray was an excellent driver, however, the curbs on that road were endless. The heavy rains didn't help the situation.

There were a couple of cars heading for the party. Trees began to fall and many of the guests began to return home way before the party began.

Those people were driving too fast without thinking of the other driver. That is when Ray and Anne crashed....

When Ray and Anne had the car accident, Anne was so injured that she fell into a coma.

Years passed but Ray did not stop visiting his wife at the hospital. Even though almost everyone, including the doctors, had given up hope, he remained faithful to Anne.

He always prayed that she would one day recover. Every time he visited her, he began talking to her, recounting all those beautiful moments they spent with each other.

One day, when he showed her the video of their wedding day, she slowly began to move her hand.

She whispered his name and began gaining consciousness. Several weeks after she had woken up, she had fully recovered and was finally allowed to leave the hospital for good.

When the couple left, she told Ray that she heard his voice while she was in a coma and that it was his voice that was the greatest aid in helping her to return to consciousness.

Chapter 60

Love letters from an Enchanted Island

In 1970, Ramon Rivera moved from Puerto Rico to New York City. The migration wasn't easy for the young man. He became terribly homesick. He missed his hometown and the company of his friends.

To distract himself, Ramon began searching for a potential pen friend from his homeland.

He found a woman called Alicia Castro from Puerto Rico. She was interested in establishing some correspondence with him.

The two slowly got to know each other, with one letter after another.

A year later, the two had fallen in love with each other, without having ever met. It took seven years for Alicia and Ramon to meet. They met for the first time, in Central Park.

Guess what? Their first meeting was the day before their wedding. The two got married and had eight children.

Chapter 61

The Farewell Gift

Michael was diagnosed with lung cancer. He had only six weeks left to live. It was a shocking diagnosis, but Michael decided to use the time he had left to make all the necessary arrangements for his wife Lourdes, with whom he had been married for 30 years.

He cashed out his pension and used the money to pay off the house they were living in. The second step was to arrange a trip for his wife Lourdes and the rest of the family to Spain.

When they visited a specific church in Spain, a priest was already waiting for the family. It was in this church that Lourdes' parents had married more than 50 years ago.

On that day, Michael and Lourdes renewed their wedding vows and had the most beautiful day.

After Michael had died, his wife Lourdes discovered that he hid hundreds of post-it notes around the entire house, shortly after they arrived from Spain.

Throughout the course of many months, she found one note after another. The notes are beautiful and very personal declarations.

Those notes were meant to encourage Lourdes in this difficult time.

Michael also reminded his wife in these notes to fully enjoy every aspect of life. He wanted Lourdes to sell his car and to move on with her life.

It was the most heartwarming farewell gift one could ever imagine.

Chapter 62

The Artistry Classes

Charles is a make-up artist who frequently holds makeup artistry classes at the local community college. Usually, most of his students are middle-aged housewives who want to fine-tune their makeup skills.

One morning, Charles held a class that would be attended by men as well. Only one man showed up.

The new student was a gentleman in his best years with a seemingly unlimited interest in makeup artistry.

He was strong with the idea to learn as much as he possibly could. He wouldn't stop until he was satisfied with the result of his work.

Conceivably, the man was the number one subject of conversation when the other women were alone. Rumors quickly started to spread.

Was he perhaps a transvestite? Why else would he attend such a class? The community college was in a conservative rural area, which is why the other participants were quite doubtful of the man's intentions.

Throughout the lessons, the man carefully listened and wrote everything down he learned.

When the classes were slowly coming to an end, the outer attendees simply could not hide their curiosity any longer.

When they finally asked him why he was so interested in makeup artistry, he gave the most inspiring beautiful reply:

He said, "You know, my beloved wife partially lost her eyesight because of diabetes.

She's no longer able to apply her makeup. I think she's beautiful, even more so without makeup.

She knows this and I tell her every day. But the thing is this, she simply feels not comfortable leaving the house without make-up.

She never went outside without wearing any makeup-up. Seeing the love of my life like this makes me sad.

So, I decided to take this course to surprise her! I do not only want to learn how to apply her makeup; I want her to wear the most beautiful make-up, so her inner beauty also shines on the outside."

Everyone got up from their sits and began to clap their hands. They thought that this guy was special. He was attending class to help his wife. They also felt ashamed because they thought so many ugly things about this wonderful individual.

Chapter 63

Love Is not just a four-letter word

Love isn't always the answer. It doesn't always conquer that emptiness in your life. Yet, many lack a clear understanding of what love is.

Some people idolize it as the answer to everything. The be-all and end-all solution to their problems. As a result, our relationships with the person we care about suffer.

Therefore, love is not enough…

An unrealistic understanding of the concept of love can cause us quite some trouble.

What happens when we overestimate the power of love? It can be seen all around us.

When we think that love is everything we need, it's likely that our relationships lack existential ingredients.

Love alone cannot compensate for a negligence of existential concepts such as patience, compromise, and mutual respect.

If, on the other hand, we understand that love really is not always enough, we also understand that maintaining a relationship takes effort. When we realize that love alone cannot solve every problem; we are more willing to confront the underlying issues firsthand.

We do not simply expect that love solves all our problems. It doesn't do that at all. All it does is cloud our perception about the situation. Before you realize it, relationships that are solely based upon love start to fall apart.

It's entirely possible that we fall in love with someone we're not compatible with. In the best case, we fall in love with someone who's just too different from us. This person might have other dreams and ambitions about life.

In the worst scenario, we fall for some truly dysfunctional characters that are abusive, manipulative, or narcissistic in nature. These are most likely people that do not treat us with the same respect we treat them.

For this reason, when evaluating a partner's compatibility, heart and mind must work together. It might feel great if you have fallen head over heels in love. But guess what, having butterflies in your stomach is simply not enough.

When it comes to your compatibility, you will also have to consider the plain facts. The way that person treats you. How their dreams are comparable to your own wishes. How your partner treats others.

Love does not overcome relationship problems

So, we've fallen head over heels in love. We get to know another person and we begin to get a more realistic picture of them. We start to realize that our partner is just another human being with faults, problems, and weaknesses. In most cases, this is a very natural process. In fact, this might be the necessary requirement to truly accept the significant other for who they are.

In some cases, however, this process is not so healthy. This is the case when we think that our love for the other person will solve relationship problems. We think love helps us to find a way to work things out.

We wholeheartedly believe that our boundless love will aid us to overcome the differences.

However, nothing changes. None of your relationship problems are solved. None of the negative or abusive behaviors of your partner cease the only thing that love changes is the way we feel about relationship problems.

It won't solve them, but it does make us feel better about them. There's a big difference between solving a problem and deluding oneself into accepting it.

Remember that the word love is not just letters put together.

That word is easily spoken, and misused.

We like to hear it because it makes us feel good. It creates lots of comfort. Especially when it comes from the person you care.

When hearing that word for the first time, one can be truly misled.

It is the case with all words, they are the unmanifested expressions of ideas and concepts. Only actions can make them real.

It takes a lot more than just words to truly love someone. Some people say they love us, but they do not act upon their words. Their actions do not coincide with their words.

The word love is not going to fix you at all.

Always keep in mind that love does not automatically restart a new life as soon as someone tells you that she or he loves you.

The mistakes committed in the past will not be undone. The pain about unresolved issues will not fade.

Ultimately, love is not going to fix you. Just because you love someone does not mean you become a better person. Being loved by someone else will also not make you a better person.

It is certainly true that a relationship can help someone to start living up. The situation is not solved. It might even get worse as days go by.

We also must keep in mind that sooner or later all the exhilarating and overjoyed feelings of the early stages will make room for something new. Before you notice it, reality will stop, and it will take hold. That's the point when you realize that you are still the same person that you were before.

Love inspires us to be better, that is true. It will help you to strive for our growth as a person. Eventually, love alone cannot effect that change. Love is not enough to live your true potential. You alone have it in your hands to be more than you are today.

Sometimes you think that love justifies sacrificing yourself. That is so wrong.

Love requires compromise. Even more so, it takes sacrifices to maintain a healthy relationship. That is the wonderful thing about love. It makes us care for the needs of another person. After all, we want our partner to feel just as great as we do. For this reason, we are willing to give up something that is our own to share it with someone else.

Sacrificing your own needs, wishes and desires is a natural part of any relationship. In fact, if such a harmony between giving and taking cannot be established, the relationship is bound to fail.

Nevertheless, love should not be taken as justification for sacrifices. It should not be the cause for you to sacrifice your dreams and ambitions just for the sake of another person.

If you must give up everything that you stand for, your dignity and individuality, then it might be a one-sided relationship. If you must sacrifice yourself just to be with someone, it had better raise a red flag.

Do not think that love is always peaches and cream...

Love isn't just bright sunshine. It isn't just pure heaven and happiness. Love is more than that. It is frustration, it is forgiveness. Love is your ability to accept another person passionately. It gives you strength to stand on this person's side even when a storm sweeps across their life, destroying everything.

True love is when you stick together during the ugly moments of life just as much as you did during the enjoyable times.

Love isn't always enough. It's not going to replace hard work, dedication, and mutual respect. It is the very structure of a relationship.

Love is the start of something beautiful. Yet, the foundation of a relationship requires much more than just love. It needs to be molded and shaped. It will have to stand the trial of fire, water, and air. Only if two people are willing to accept that love is not enough, a long-lasting and healthy relationship can be established.

I want you to always remember that it's very important not to let love consume you. It shouldn't be our most important priority in life. It shouldn't be allowed to serve as justification for sacrifice.

Glossary

Autobiography – a detailed description or account of the storyteller's own life.

Biography – a detailed description or account of someone's life.

Captivity narrative – a story in which the protagonist is captured and describes their experience with the culture of their captors.

Epic – a very long narrative poem, often written about a hero or heroine and their exploits.

Epic poem – a lengthy story of heroic exploits in the form of a poem.

Fable – a didactic story, often using animal characters who behave like people.

Fantasy – a story about characters that may not be realistic and about events that could not really happen.

Folk tale – an old story which has been passed down orally and which reveals the customs of a culture.

Historical fiction – stories which take place in real historical settings, and which often feature real historical figures and events, but which center around fictional characters and/or events.

Legend – a story that is based on fact but often includes exaggerations about the hero.

Memoir – like an autobiography, except that memoirs generally deal with specific events in the life of the author.

Myth – an ancient story often meant to explain the mysteries of life or nature.

News – information on current events which is presented by print, broadcast, Internet, or word of mouth to a third party or mass audience.

Nonlinear narrative – a story whose plot does not conform to conventional chronology, causality, and/or perspective.

Novel – a long, written narrative, normally in prose, which describes fictional characters and events, usually in the form of a sequential story.

Novella – a written, fictional, prose narrative normally longer than a short story but shorter than a novel.

Parable – a succinct, didactic story, in prose or verse, which illustrates one or more instructive lessons or principles.

Play – a story that is told mostly through dialogue and is meant to be performed on stage.

Quest narrative – a story in which the characters must achieve a goal. This includes some illness narratives.

Realistic fiction – stories which portray fictional characters, settings, and events that could exist in real life.

Short story – a brief story that usually focuses on one character and one event.

Tall tale – a humorous story that tells about impossible happenings, exaggerating the hero's accomplishments.

Genre - A literary genre is a category of literary composition. Genres may be determined by literary technique, tone, content, or even (as in the case of fiction) length. The distinctions between genres and categories are flexible and loosely defined, often with subgroups.

The most general genres in literature are (in loose chronological order) epic, tragedy, comedy, and creative nonfiction. They can all be in the form of prose or poetry. Additionally, a genre such as satire, allegory or pastoral might appear in any of the above, not only as a subgenre (see below), but as a mixture of genres. Finally, they are defined by the general cultural movement of the historical period in which they were composed.

Genre should not be confused with age categories, by which literature may be classified as either adult, young adult, or children's. They also must not be confused with format, such as graphic novel or picture book.

Action fiction Adventure Comic Crime Docufiction Epistolary Erotic Fiction Fantasy Gothic Historical Horror Magic realism Mystery Nautical Paranoid Philosophical Picaresque Political Psychological Romance Saga Satire Science Speculative Superhero Thriller Urban Western List of writing genres

Narration - is the use of a written or spoken commentary to convey a story to an audience. Narration encompasses a set of techniques through which the creator of the story presents their story, including:

Narrative point of view: the perspective or type of personal or non-personal "lens" through which a story is communicated

Narrative voice- the format or type presentational form through which a story is communicated

Narrative time- the grammatical placement of the story's timeframe in the past, the present, or the future.

Narrator - is a personal character or a non-personal voice that the creator, author, of the story develops to deliver information to the audience, particularly about the plot.

In the case of most written narratives such as novels, short stories, poems, etc. the narrator typically functions are to convey the story in its entirety. The narrator may be a voice devised by the author as an anonymous, non-personal, or stand-alone entity; as the author as a character; or as some other fictional or non-fictional character appearing and participating within their own story. The narrator is considered participant if he/she is a character within the story, and non-participant if he/she is an implied character or an omniscient or semi-omniscient being or voice that merely relates the story to the audience without being involved in the actual events. Some stories have multiple narrators to illustrate the storylines of various characters at the same, similar, or different times, thus allowing a more complex, non-singular point of view.

Narration encompasses not only who tells the story, but also how the story is told for example, by using stream of consciousness or unreliable narration.

In traditional literary narratives such as novels, short stories, and memoirs, narration is a required story element; in other types of chiefly non-literary narratives, such as plays, television shows, video games, and films, narration is merely optional.

References

1. Browns, Julie, ed. (1997). Ethnicity and the American Short Story. New York: Garland.

2. Goyet, Florence (2014). The Classic Short Story, 1870-1925: Theory of a Genre. Cambridge U.K.: Open Book Publishers.

3. Gelfant, Blanche; Lawrence Graver, eds. (2000). The Columbia Companion to the Twentieth-Century American Short Story. Columbia University Press.

4. Hart, James; Phillip Leininger, eds. (1995). Oxford Companion to American Literature. Oxford University Press.

5. Ibáñez, José R; José Francisco Fernández; Carmen M. Bretones, eds. (2007)., Contemporary Debates on the Short Story. Bern: Lang.

6. Iftekharrudin, Farhat; Joseph Boyden; Joseph Longo; Mary Rohrberger, eds. (2003). Postmodern Approaches to the Short Story. Westport, CN: Praeger.

7. Kennedy, Gerald J., ed. (2011). Modern American Short Story Sequences: Composite Fictions and Fictive Communities. Cambridge: Cambridge University Press.

8. Lohafer, Susan (2003). Reading for Storyness: Preclosure Theory, Empirical Poetics, and Culture in the Short Story. Baltimore, MD: Johns Hopkins University Press.

9. Magill, Frank, ed. (1997). Short Story Writers. Pasadena, California: Salem Press.

10. Patea, Viorica, ed. (2012). Short Story Theories: A Twenty-First-Century Perspective. Amsterdam: Rodopi.
11. Scofield, Martin, ed. (2006). The Cambridge Introduction to the American Short Story. Cambridge: Cambridge University Press.
12. Watson, Noelle, ed. (1994). Reference Guide to Short Fiction. Detroit: St. James Press.
13. Winther, Per; Jakob Lothe; Hans H. Skei, eds. (2004). The Art of Brevity: Excursions in Short Fiction Theory and Analysis. Columbia, SC: University of South Carolina Press.

Norma Iris Pagan Morales was born in Ponce, Puerto Rico. She comes from a very lovable family. Her parents, Juan Jose Pagan Rodriguez, and Digna Morales Figueroa, now deceased, always helped her with her projects as a writer and teaching career.

Norma had three siblings, Adelin Milagros Pagan Morales, Juan Jose Pagan Morales, and Julio Manuel Pagan Morales. Julio Manuel Pagan Morales died on September 19, 1998, and my dear sister Adelin Milagros Pagan Morales died on February 17, 2023.

Norma did all her academic studies in New York City, Puerto Rico, and Canada. She worked in the City of New York Police Department. As an Educator, she worked in New York City Bd. Of Education as an English Teacher, in Puerto Rico Bd. of Education as an English teacher and in the Puerto Rico Army National.

She has teaching certifications for English as a Second Language and Teaching English as a Foreign Language.

She had published seventeen books: Proud of My Puerto Rican Bequest, ¿Porque Soy Boricua? Poemas del Alma, Art in Written Form, A Baffling Short Stories Collection, On Job in the Big Apple, Puerto Rican Soldiers Serving with Pride, Nature's Rage in the Caribbean, Boricua de Pura Cepa, You are the One, The Unfaithfuls, Christopher Columbus, Violence in the City, Poemas Tiernos, Mis Raices, My Little Sister and Two Strangers.